Other Books
By Larry M. Greer

Appalachian Trail After Dark
American Neanderthal
Does God Play Golf?
The Ghost of Keowee
Heaven is in Union County
Soft Target
Tomb Society

Coming soon...
Virginia
(a sequel to *The Author's Woman*)

The Author's Woman

Copyright © 2018 by Larry M. Greer
Printed in the United States of America

All rights reserved. Except as permitted under U.S. Copyright Act of 1976, no part of this publication may be reproduced, distributed or transmitted in any form or by any means, or stored in a database or retrieval system, without the prior written permission of the author.

This is a work of fiction. Names, characters, places and incidents either are the product of the author's imagination or are used fictitiously. Any resemblance to actual persons living or dead, events, or locales is entirely coincidental.

ISBN – 13:
978-1719236867

ISBN – 10:
1719236860

Cover design by Rick Schroeppel,
Elm Street Design Studio

Acknowledgements

To John Thornton, Regents Professor, Emeritus, University of North Texas. John spent countless hours reading, editing, and providing wise counsel on both content and composition. Because of his scrupulous attention to detail, The Author's Woman is well 'turned-out'. Many thanks, John.

No book is complete before it is thoroughly vetted by a good editor. While an author can spin a tale, an editor's job is to polish the story. Carol Browning has spent countless hours polishing The Author's Woman and preparing it for the publisher. Thank you, Carol!

The Author's Woman

By
Larry M. Greer

Chapter 1

Many writers have talked about how excruciating the initial process of a novel can be. They recount tossing and turning in their sleep as they struggle to develop the plot. However, even as a novice writer, Champ would sit at his computer in the wee hours of the night, when all the intrusions of the day were forgotten, and a story would seem to ooze from the right side of his brain, flow through his fingers and splash onto the page.

Now with a dozen or more titles under his belt, a healthy income from his writing, and a bitter divorce behind him, he was free to live where he wanted, to write what he wanted, and free to do something different. It was time for a fresh start, both for his personal life and his writing.

This was his favorite time of day, actually favorite time of night, when the moon cast a silvery patina over the waters of the Florida Gulf and silence was only broken by the gliding of shimmery waves onto the white sand. He had been pacing his condo for several hours as he absorbed this new freedom. On impulse, he pulled a book from his copious library and settled into the hammock on his lanai to lose himself in a novel. Not coincidentally, his hand had landed on Michener's 'Alaska'. He had read this volume and many of Michener's other tales more than once. Champ felt that Michener's books were authentic and credible because he frequently relocated to the site of his story. This fact circled around the back of Champ's brain as he read his first words.

Suddenly Michener's habit of moving to his story's setting had new meaning for Champ. The book slid to the lanai floor and he sat bolt upright. He was tired of living in Florida's sticky, humid climate. He too, could benefit from a change of venue.

Recently he had seen a feature article on The History Channel about prohibition and moonshine. The narrator relayed tales of an area in the Blue Ridge Mountains of South Carolina, known by locals as The Dark Corner. Although local mountain families had been making moonshine for over two hundred years, the area gained its infamy in the 1940's with the advent of prohibition and revenuers. Although prohibition has long since ended, the distillation and local sale of corn liquor remains an illegal occupation. According to The History Channel story, it is still being produced deep in those Blue Ridge Mountains. The segment of the program that particularly caught his attention told about the life of an elusive moonshiner who had gained hero status among local residents.

This story of Tom Tatum captured his imagination and mingled with the idea of living where the story unfolded. All night those two thoughts churned through his subconscious. And when the first rays of dawn painted the Atlantic gold and fuchsia, the fresh start he needed became obvious.

With the help of Google Earth and the internet, it did not take long to locate a realtor in the small town of Salem, South Carolina. Champ envisioned a residence completely different from the cold, industrial high-rise that was his current surroundings. Given his vivid description of the type of house he was looking to rent, the realtor quickly recommended a "perfect little log cabin" about a mile off Gap Hill Road. He impetuously agreed to rent this cozy cabin, sight-unseen, and that should have been a warning sign. But Champ was hell-bent on a wild new adventure.

****

It was his first day at the ancient weathered cabin, which he had leased at the modest rate of $200 a month. It was literally a two-room cabin…a bedroom and a second room that could definitely not be described as a great room. More like a 'common area'. However, to be fair, it did include a rustic wood-burning fireplace and a kitchen at one end. It was the real deal! When Mr. Realtor bragged that it was estimated to be over a hundred years old, Champ thought he must have subtracted numerous decades from the actual time it was constructed. The yard, if you wanted to call it that, was all natural with a small stream bubbling down the hill on one side of the cabin. The stream was bordered on the upper bank by a hedge of giant poplar trees. The cabin was framed on the opposite side by a ring of massive, moss-covered boulders. So, despite its obvious age, it did possess a quaint nature. One detail Mr. Realtor neglected to mention before Champ signed the lease was the lack of indoor 'facilities'. He chuckled when he thought of what a life-change it was to do his business in a massive spa-like bathroom one week; and to freeze his ass off on a splintered wooden outhouse the next.

As a writer, the most appropriate adjective that came to Champ's mind when describing the cabin was 'primitive'. He had discovered that his water source came from the small spring up the ravine that bubbled up from beneath a cluster of Mountain Laurel. At some time in the recent past, a pipe had been installed which deposited the fresh ice-cold water into a cistern behind the cabin. Lucky for Champ, a hot water heater had also been added to the cabin's amenities.

The final complaint he had about his new abode was the lack of natural light. The entire 150-foot cabin contained four small grimy windows. However, he reminded himself, this was an adventure and he thought about what Michener must have endured to write his masterpieces. "So...here I go," thought Champ.

It did not take long for him to settle in. He enjoyed all the changes he was experiencing. In Florida, seasons were mostly elusive. Here, he could feel fall in the air. The days were growing shorter and the evenings much cooler. That particular evening his living room felt chilly. So, he decided to cheer up the space with a cozy fire.

He set his computer on a small table in the corner of the kitchen and positioned a floor lamp near the table for sufficient light. After surveying his arrangement, he felt confident that this was where he would be most productive. He nestled a small space heater under the table for added warmth and decided that he had created a very cozy environment to foster inspiration.

As had been his habit in the past, Champ did not sit down to write until well after midnight. It was these wee hours of the day that his creativity and imagination were at their best. However, writing at night deep in the Carolina mountains was a very different experience. There was no evidence of light pollution in the inky black sky. And the silence of the woods at night was deafening. That night, a light rain peppered the rusty tin roof. Champ was beginning to realize that he was uncomfortable with the solitude. Although he did not miss the cacophony of noises from busy streets below his St. Petersburg condo, night sounds in the mountains were completely foreign. Tonight, he did not even have the comfort white noise from his TV. That reminded him of yet another detail Mr. Realtor had forgotten to mention...the lack of a phone signal. The first item on his list the next morning was to see if he could talk the owner into running a landline to the cabin. Next on the list would be having a satellite dish installed.

The evening's chill was not totally abated by Champ's space heater and fireplace, so he found my heavy sweater and stoked the fire with a few more logs.

It was now one-thirty a.m. and Champ set about concentrating on the nuances of how to introduce his protagonist, Tom Tatum. Not two minutes into this process, he heard what sounded like a creak on his front step. He listened again to see if his imagination was working overtime in this unfamiliar environment. Chills went up his back and he sat frozen in his chair. Again, he heard what sounded like the weight of a footstep on the sagging wooden step. This time was certain it was not his imagination. He had noticed the last stair was sagging and creaky when he had moved his belongings into the cabin. The sound he had made on those stairs was identical to what he had just heard. In this ink-black night with nothing but a two-hundred-year-old door between him and whoever was outside, he was scared shitless!

Silently, he swiveled in his chair, convinced there would soon be a knock on the door. But no knock came. He wanted to creep across the room and peer out the window, but there was no outside porch light. Another miss on his part when moving in. And another item to add to his list for tomorrow...that is if he lived till tomorrow. He crept to the front door and without opening it. projected the deepest, loudest voice he could muster, "Is there anyone out there?"

Silence! The only thing he heard was rain dripping from the old tin roof.

Chapter 2

Champ attempted to replace panic with logic, as he pondered the options. A dog? He had not seen one since moving in, and besides most dogs would not have been heavy enough to make the step squeak. His next thought was that it could be a bear. He was told not to leave his trash out, as it encouraged bears to wander into yards and make a mess of the garbage. The clerk at the hardware store in Salem strongly recommended he purchase a lockable bear box for his trash. This too, would go on his list for tomorrow's errands.

He didn't really think there was a bear on his porch, as he did not hear additional sounds that a rummaging animal might make. Champ's next thought was more frightening...a person who might be intent on mischief or worse. So much for remaining rational!

The silence continued and finally he returned to his writing table but could not shift his mind back to Tom Tatum. This struck him as ironic. In an effort to emulate his idol, James Michener, he had relocated to the setting of his story. Now, instead of writing about this remote, lawless area, he was personally experiencing the fear he had intended to paint for his readers. Perhaps his imagination was on overdrive in these unfamiliar surroundings.

Champ found that he could not concentrate, so he pulled the shades over the four windows and settled into his La-Z-Boy near the fire and attempted a nap. At five a.m. he gave up. He made himself a cup of coffee and added two more items to his list of necessities for this cabin...a gun and a porch light (and of course an electrician).

Even after last night's scare, the habit of writing late at night was still a part of his author's DNA, so this left the daylight hours for errands and exploring. As he headed toward Salem, his curiosity led him down, and back out of, some less traveled roads. He had been cautioned not to venture too far into the woods, especially into the dark hollows where a mountain stream might flow. It was good advice, so Champ made sure he could easily backtrack.

There was much history hidden in these mountains. Champ spent a great deal of his time researching. He discovered that Immigrants settled in these mountains prior to the Civil War. At that time, they were primarily poor Irish and English families. They cultivated relationships with indigenous Indians and learned that corn grew well in the river-bottom lands. They quickly realized the rich soil made the perfect corn for liquor. Eventually, the government recognized the revenue opportunities and implemented a tax on liquor sales. Not surprisingly, Champ learned that this did not sit well with the independent immigrants of The Dark Corner, so they moved their stills deeper into the isolated mountains and concealed their moonshine operations. Enforcing this new tax opportunity became increasingly difficult. The Dark Corner became a lawless part of the South and more often than not, disputes were settled at the point of a gun. Lawmen knew they were risking their lives when venturing into the mountains in pursuit of law-breakers.

It did not take Champ long to realize that, in many ways, the reputation garnered nearly a century earlier in The Dark Corner, remained. Locals were guarded and very private. He decided that if he wanted to assimilate into the culture, he needed to blend in. So, he had purchased a battered old Ford pickup with a windowless locking shell secured to the truck bed. This shell served to protect his meager belongings and was a perfect place to secure his new mountain bike. In Florida, he had enjoyed the numerous bike trails and flat country roads, but in this new terrain, his old beach bike was not suitable. So, he bit the bullet and invested in a used, but well-appointed mountain bike. However, after the previous night, he decided it would be better stored inside the cabin.

His errands were completed by early afternoon and he decided that a warm fire and a nice nap were in order. He awoke refreshed several hours later. With last night's fear abated, he donned the used work jeans and tee-shirt purchased at Goodwill and decided to take his new bike for a spin. Not knowing the area well, he flipped a coin and took a left out of the driveway onto the narrow, paved mountain road that ran along the Big Estatoee River. It was a beautiful warm October afternoon. Shorter days and cooler evenings had painted leaves the burgundies, tangerines and lemon colors of Autumn.

He plodded up the hill, learning the complicated gears of the bike as he rode. The unmistakable roar of Harleys sounded somewhere above him on the mountain and interrupted the silence of the afternoon. He rode for at least an hour, soaking in the sights and aromas of his new environment. He had worked up a significant sweat climbing the last hill and realized that he had probably bitten off more than he could chew. Out of nowhere, four Harleys whizzed past him, offering a wave as they passed. Champ nearly lost control of his bike. It was definitely time to turn around and coast back down the mountain!

Champ approached a sharp curve in the road, intending to turn around at the top. When he slowed to turn, he was startled at the sight of a Harley gathering smack dab at the apex of where two roads met. Bikers gathered outside of a ramshackle old building, perched in the middle of the apex. Flying above this rundown shack were both an American flag and the infamous Confederate flag. It was obvious that this was the source of the distinctive roar of Harley motorcycles he had heard earlier. There must have been thirty to forty people gathered outside this bar, drinking beer and visiting. Some were sitting on makeshift milk crates, or on tree stumps near the building. Others were admiring the chrome and gadgets of the expensive 'Hogs'. Champ realized that he must have been gaping at the sight and decided he'd better head out before anyone spotted him. It was at that exact moment that a couple of the guys called out to him. "Hey, come join us for a beer." Another chided, "We welcome any type of biker here at Bob's Place." Several laughed and motioned for Champ to join them. He decided it was better to take them up on their offer than put his tail between his legs and run.

Most dressed the part of a biker...leather chaps, do-rags and studded jackets. Some sported beards and others were totally bald. Fearing that he looked like a geek, compared to them, he tried nonchalance, smoothly dismounting his mountain bike and leaning it against a wooden post. He was very careful to park it a significant distance from any of the posh 'Hogs'. He ambled over to the two guys that had called to him and offered a handshake.

"Thanks for the invite. Name's Champ."

"And I'm Bill. This is my girlfriend Carol and my friend Chuck."

They made pleasantries and Champ inquired where they were from. Bill responded that they had ridden up from Greenville about 50 miles southeast. Champ was pleasantly surprised with the welcoming nature of the conversation.

"How about you Champ?" Bill asked.

"Well, I just moved from St. Petersburg a few weeks ago and rented a cabin not far from here."

Champ continued to probe, attempting to learn more. "Are you from the Greenville area, Bill?"

"Yes, Both Carol and I are lawyers and we escape the city and the stress of the job on our bikes most weekends. We've found it a great way to unwind. There are twelve of us in the group...all lawyers. I'll bet that bit of information blows your stereotype of Harley Hogs!"

"You're right. Guess I never thought about the diversity of Harley enthusiasts," Champ admitted.

"Champ, they got cold beer inside for two bucks. Let me get you one," Bill offered.

When Bill came back with the beer, he asked, "So what's your line of work, Champ?"

"Well, like you, I have a J.D. behind my name. But I found it was not for me. A number of years ago I walked away from a lucrative litigation career to follow my dream to write fiction."

"So, you're an author?" asked another man who had been listening into the exchange.

Before I could respond, Bill exclaimed, "Well I'll be dammed. You must be the famous author, Champ Covington! I own every one of your novels. You spin quite a tale." He turned to his girlfriend. "Carol, can you believe it? Champ Covington right here in this beer joint in The Dark Corner!"

Before Champ knew it, a crowd of bikers had gathered around him asking questions. Suddenly he no longer felt like the geek he had minutes earlier. Champ was flattered to find myself in this back-road biker bar, being recognized by many strangers. "Goes to show, you can't judge bikers by their outfits," Champ chuckled to himself. "Lawyers just like me...who'd have thunk it?"

Champ lingered, chewing the fat with the group until he realized that if he didn't leave soon, he'd be heading down the mountain in the dark. But before he departed, he had a question for Bill. On his way up the hill that afternoon, Champ decided that he needed a dog...both for security and companionship. A good dog could be his alarm system and keep at bay whatever went bump in the night.

"Hey Bill, I'm interested in finding a good four-legged companion while I'm here in South Carolina. Do you know of an animal shelter up here or any of the locals that might have a dog for sale?"

"Oh yeah, you'll find some of the locals sitting on the bar stools inside. Almost all of the locals have at least one dog it seems. Just ask any of them and I'm sure you will find someone who will have one they would be willing to part with; especially if you are willing to pay." Bill grinned at this.

Because of the friendly reception at this hole-in-the-wall bar, Champ now felt brave enough to head inside the dingy shack. He opened the dilapidated screen door and just stood in the doorway. His eyes needed a moment to adjust to the windowless room; and his olfactory senses needed time to become accustomed to the moldy aroma. The only light streamed in through a second screen door at the opposite end of the long room. He had to stifle a laugh when he spotted two hefty Brahama chickens pecking at the filthy floor. Unlike the upscale clubs he was used to in Florida, this establishment had no big screen TV; no USB charging stations; no scantily clad bar maids; and the only power source was a naked electrical outlet into which the two beer coolers were plugged.

The guys sitting at the stools inside this bar were not part of the biker crowd. They were dressed in dirty coveralls and thread-bare tee-shirts. Although Champ's attire was more like theirs, he felt gussied up in his clean jeans. Next time he came up here, he would lose the creases in his jeans and make sure his tee-shirt included some of the red clay soil they were so proud of in these parts.

Several of the locals were engrossed in a discussion of logging issues. As he leaned over between two of them to get a beer, he smiled and interrupted their conversation to ask if they knew anyone that might have a good watch dog for sale. An old man, probably in his eighties, gave Champ a toothless grin and replied,

"I sho do. He da one at da end in dat huntin' get-up, sittin' on two stools."

"Could you tell me his name?"

"He go by da name Big Bongo."

"Big Bongo, now that's a handle," Champ responded, attempting to fit in.

"Big Bongo, he's a mighty good hunter. If anyone 'round here knows dogs, he do."

Champ thanked the old man and took his beer, easing his way through the crowd. By a stroke of luck there was an empty seat next to the enormous man. As Champ approached, he could see why the man needed two stools on which to perch. He must have weighed between two-fifty and three hundred pounds. He was wearing hunter's coveralls and at least eight empty beer cans sat in front of him on the bar. Champ was not sure he'd ever seen a man that big. If the man had a neck, it was not visible. His head, covered by a frizzy afro, nested right on top of the broadest shoulders Champ had ever seen on a human being.

Champ was hesitant about approaching the giant and even more unsure of whether it was appropriate for a stranger to call him by his nickname. Champ assumed 'Big Bongo' was a nickname.

The man sat very still, staring into space. Since he was not engaged in conversation with anyone, Champ decided to live dangerously and introduce himself.

"Sir, the man down the other end of the bar said maybe you might know where I could get me a good watch dog."

At first, Champ thought the man had not heard him. But then, very slowly he began to swivel his monstrous head in Champ's direction. Even in the dingy light of the bar, Champ could see that the man's eyes looked jaundiced. He neither smiled nor blinked. It was like he was staring straight through Champ. Yet again within 24 hours, he was scared shitless!

The surprises at this mountain bar never ended. In a very uncharacteristically soft voice the man asked, "Did you say something about a dog?"

Champ introduced himself and the large man told Champ that most people just called him Big Bongo.

The soft-spoken nature of this giant gave Champ a little more confidence, so he ventured on with his inquiry about a dog.

"I just moved here from Florida. I've rented the old Dexter cabin off Gap Hill Road. It is a bit more remote than I'm used to and thought I could use a good watch dog."

"Well for the right man," he replied slowly. He looked Champ up and down before proceeding. Evidently, he had decided in Champ's favor. "I may have just the right dog for you. Name is Sam. He's a Black and Tan Coonhound, 'bout ten years old. He's too old to hunt anymore, but he can still howl the daylights out and loves to just lie on the porch. He looks lazy, but nothin' escapes that hound!"

"Big Bongo, do you suppose I could try him out and see if we get along?" Champ asked.

"Well you look like a nice enough fellow. Maybe I could drop him off in the next day or two. What's your name again?"

"Champ, Champ Covington."

"You the fellow they were makin' a fuss over out there? Some kind of book writer?"

Champ had to smile, "That would be me."

"God, I have never met nobody famous."

Champ laughed and responded, "Well maybe you still haven't."

They drank another beer together (making it about ten for Big Bongo). Champ decided he was really very friendly after you got to know him. He was feeling comfortable by this time and so his writer's curiosity kicked in. Champ asked Bongo how he got his nickname. Again, there was no immediate response. Then he leaned close to Champ's face and replied, "Got it in prison". Both because of his proximity now and because of his unabashed admission of prison time, Champ's confidence evaporated.

"Why…why did they give you that name?" Champ stammered.

He didn't appear to notice Champ's nervousness. "Well it was 'cause I had a set of bongo drums an' I was always beatin' on 'em."

Champ let out an uneasy chuckle and forged ahead. "You know writers are always curious. Sometimes to our detriment. You mind if I ask why you were in prison?"

With this question, Big Bongo leaned even closer and whispered into Champ's ear. "I was sent up on a murder charge."

There had to be a good story here, so Champ forged ahead.

"But here you are, and I assume a free man?"

"'Dat's right," was his only response.

Against his better judgement Champ continued. "So how did you get out?" He was dying to hear his answer.

Bongo moved uncomfortably close to me again. Champ could smell beer on Bongo's breath as he whispered in his ear.

"I got out on a technicality."

"A technicality?" Champ echoed.

"Yeah, they never found the body."

Bongo studied Champ's reaction, but never batted an eye.

With this revelation, Champ decided it was definitely time he head home. As graciously as he could, he bid farewell to Big Bongo and backed out of the bar, making his way to his bike as nonchalantly as possible. As he sped his bike down the mountain, countless thoughts raced through his head. What an afternoon that had been!

Champ reached the bottom of the last hill just as sun was kissing the mountain peaks goodbye. As dusk emerged, so did the memories of the previous night. What kind of man had he just befriended? And he was coming to Champ's cabin! Champ was beginning to question the wisdom of his 'fresh start'.

Chapter 3

Once more Champ sat at his computer and attempted to write. However, both the late-night visitor and his encounter with Big Bongo left him slightly off balance. He simply could not concentrate. To ease his mind, he thoroughly checked the steps and the entire front porch the following morning. There were no animal tracks or even human footprints on, or near the porch. Bear or human, something heavy had stepped onto that top stair. He could not ignore the probability that someone had approached his cabin and come as close as his front door. Now, even in broad daylight, his nerves were on edge.

Big Bongo had promised to bring Sam for a trial run either this afternoon or tomorrow. Champ certainly hoped it would be sooner than later. Bongo had seemed likable enough, despite his prison revelations. Had he been falsely accused, or did he have a violent side? It certainly sounded like he had confessed to murder. Remembering the smug look on his face when whispering that they had never found the body, still gave Champ chills. He decided it would not be wise to pursue this subject with him any further.

Sunday morning the skies were clear and the temperature mild. Champ wanted to get in a few hours on his bike before settling down to some serious work on the new book. He decided to change his pattern and confine his writing to daylight hours. On Monday morning he would drive into Salem and apply for a gun permit. A dog...a gun...a porch light and a house phone. He needed all these to feel comfortable enough in this remote cabin to release the creative juices that would allow him to begin writing in earnest.

Champ turned right out of the driveway onto Gap Hill Road and felt the crisp mid-morning breeze wash over his face. He made a mental note of everything he was experiencing on this beautiful fall morning and would document it the minute he returned home in an effort to recreate for his readers, the nuances of this place.

One unique observation involved mailboxes. Each time he passed a mailbox, it sat at the beginning of a very long road with no house in sight, yet one more illustration of how much people in The Dark Corner liked their privacy. On rare occasions when he encountered someone, they would wave, but that was it. They made no effort to speak to strangers. The South's tradition of holding strangers at arm's length was rigorously exaggerated up here.

The level road allowed him to assume a more leisurely pace in order to absorb more of the experience. The sign in front of yet another long driveway read,

'Tucker Farm Lane'. This particular lane was wider than most he had observed; and the dirt path was pitted with deep ruts which looked more like they had been created by wagon wheels than car tires.

He could no longer curtail his curiosity about these long, isolated driveways, so he decided to explore this one, hoping that he would not be met at the end by a barrel of a shotgun. It was a beautiful autumn afternoon and the weather report indicated this might be one of the few remaining warm days before winter set it. He made a mental note to have a cord of wood delivered.

Champ navigated the rutted path as it meandered through what appeared to be a ravine, separating two large mountains. He found it interesting that the road did not ascend the mountain but remained level as it followed a babbling brook. In places the path became a tunnel created by thickets of Mountain Laurel. Absorbed as he was with the scenery, he did not realize that he had traveled nearly two miles down this drive. Then he noticed a woman walking in his direction. As she approached, Champ became intrigued by her attire. She wore a large bonnet which hid her face. This made it impossible to determine her age. The rest of her attire was even more unusual. Her ankle-length dress looked like she had snatched it from an Amish museum and the blue patterned material was from the same material as her bonnet.

He slowed down and nodded in recognition of her presence. She was tall for a woman and walked with a rigid gait. As we closed ranks to within a hundred feet of each other, he spotted a wisp of white hair that had escaped her bonnet. From that one observation, he took her to be an elderly woman.

When they were within earshot, he spoke and flashed his award-winning smile. She cut her eyes very briefly in Champ's direction and tipped her head in acknowledgement. He decided that she must be slightly north of eighty.

Out of respect, he continued his ride. However, he had the uncontrollable urge to turn and look back in her direction. She stood perfectly still, gazing back at him. Champ figured that he was heading in the direction of her home. Perhaps he would be wise to turn around, given the warnings he had heard about privacy in these mountains. But like an idiot, he continued.

He navigated a small bend in the road and was stunned by what he saw. Nestled in the cleavage between two mountains sat a magnificent little glen. An ancient farm house rested on a slight rise, guarding the emerald pastures below. This splendid setting must be where the old woman lived.

Suddenly, the cautions about respecting privacy hit him like a brick. Although he had not seen any 'NO

TRESPASSING' signs, he knew he had overstepped his bounds by entering this valley. Immediately Champ reversed course and peddled rapidly in the direction he had come.

The next few minutes on that time-worn path would immutably alter his future.

Chapter 4

On October 20, 1969 at the stroke of midnight, screams of pain emanated from a farm house in the tiny valley near the Big Estatoee River in Salem, South Carolina. A baby boy named Lloyd came into the world that night. The next morning, his proud father took the baby out onto the porch and laid him on the corn scale. According to the mid-wife, Lloyd Simmons weighed fourteen pounds. He was the youngest of eight children, and the last. A week after his birth, his mother died from the childbirth.

Lloyd's father, John, was left with only his oldest daughter to care for the other seven children, including baby Lloyd. This soon became too much of a burden for a young girl of thirteen. To feed his growing family, John worked full time at the saw mill and took part-time jobs as he could get them.

Little Lloyd, who was never really little, continued to grow. He would never be tall, but every part of his body appeared over-sized. An unusually thick neck was the only salvation for his excessively sized head. Even the most obnoxious classmates never considered bullying Lloyd. However, even though he was not bullied by other children, neither was he befriended by any of them. Inwardly, he considered himself a freak.

Lloyd dropped out of school at 16 and the Army was delighted with his enlistment. Because of his bulk, the running portion of boot camp was a struggle. However, when it came to strength training, he out-performed everyone else in his class. In fact, he out-performed anyone who had ever *gone* through boot camp at Fort Jackson. Some of the recruits in his company were terrified of him. His massive bulk, the constant yellow tinge to his eyes and his uncharacteristically soft voice, unnerved most people. Although he was used to people making fun of his appearance, he tolerated none of it. When he caught wind that he was the subject of gossip, the perpetrators would find themselves swaying in midair and staring into the face of Little Lloyd Simmons. After a few choice words from the soft-spoken Simmons, the soldier's collar was released, and he was pitched to the ground.

After four years in the Army, Lloyd returned home to find his father deceased and his family scattered across the South. He quickly found a job driving lumber trucks for a local timber company. But weekends were what he lived for, hunting wild game in his beloved Blue Ridge Mountains.

On opening day of deer season, his first year out of the army, he headed out before daylight, excited to get settled into his deer stand before sunrise. As he approached his stand that morning, the crack of a high-powered rifle echoed close to where he stood. It was a time-honored rule among hunters, that deer stands (set up weeks before the season opened), would be located out of range of another hunter's stand. This rifle shot was so close that Lloyd was alarmed. In the pre-dawn light, he headed in the direction from where the shot had come. Lloyd wanted to know who in the hell fired that single shot. He fully intended on giving this errant hunter a piece of his mind. Quietly he traversed the narrow logging road, with the rifle shot still ringing in his ears. Suddenly, he spotted a man dressed in hunting clothes lying face down in the leaves. Lloyd's keen observation skills, sharply honed during his army training, detected someone fleeing through the dense woods.

Again, his military training kicked in and his first concern was for the injured man on the ground. He carefully rolled the man over to determine if he was still alive. It was at just that moment, Lloyd heard more footsteps. He turned to find two men, attired in hunting gear, heading his direction.

"What's going on here? We heard a shot," one of them accused.

"I don't know. I heard the shot as well and came to see who was shooting so close to my deer stand." Lloyd responded.

"Is he alive?" one of the hunters asked.

"I don't know, but I can't detect a heartbeat." One of the two hunters bent down to examine the fallen man.

"He's definitely dead. Looks like a single rifle bullet passed clear through him."

The two hunters asked Lloyd to stay with the man while they went to their car to contact the Sheriff.

About an hour later, Lloyd was sitting at the foot of a pine tree, waiting for the hunters to return. When he spotted them, they had three lawmen in tow. They took a look at the victim and then one of the deputies asked Lloyd if he was the first one on the scene. Lloyd shared what had happened and relayed the facts as he knew them.

"That's a nice rifle you are hunting with." The deputy observed. "Is it yours?"

"Yes sir," Lloyd replied.

"I wonder where the victim's gun is?"

"I could not say, sir. It was not with him when I arrived." Lloyd responded.

That was when the miscarriage of justice took place. The deputies stood off from the hunters and huddled in hushed discussion. Periodically they glanced back at Lloyd. Still focusing on the death of a hunter, Lloyd was oblivious to the deputies' assessment of the situation, so when one of the deputies approached him and announced that he was under arrest, Lloyd was stunned.

"What in the hell are you saying? Under arrest for what?" Lloyd was alarmed at this turn of events.

"On suspicion of murder. I'll read you your rights. After that you better watch what you say, young man."

For the first time in his life, Little Lloyd Simmons was afraid.

Chapter 5

As Champ turned to leave the beautiful valley, he picked up his pace as if being chased. He had seen nothing to encourage this paranoia except numerous warnings about his propensity for poking his nose in people's business. The most memorable caution: 'You never know the secrets hidin' in these hills'.

Champ had always found it important to understand the people and become familiar with the setting of his stories. This local knowledge was critical to a story's credibility. However, he was now finding that following Michener's relocation tactic held significantly more danger than he anticipated. With previous books, he had conducted his research in the sterile environment of Google. Occasionally he would actually venture to a local library. Now, thoughts of ghostly visitors and monstrous criminals drove adrenalin throughout his body and added strength to his peddling legs.

As the sun dropped below the two mountains that cradled the small valley, and shadows lengthened, Tucker Farm Lane took on a more ominous atmosphere. Even the babbling stream alongside the road lost its comforting nature.

His entire focus was on the rutted path and its cavernous pot holes. As a result, he almost ran over the old lady as she too had turned and was heading back toward her home. He spotted her just in time so that he could make eye contact and pleasantries. But when he came within a few bike lengths of her, he was dumbfounded. The blue patterned dress and large bonnet were exactly the same, but the woman outfitted in this historic attire was not the graying eighty-year-old, but a stunningly attractive young woman in her forties. Her eyes were a rich hazel color and she had silky chestnut hair escaping in ringlets from that enormous blue bonnet. As he eased passed her he must have allowed the bewilderment to show on his face. She returned his stare with what could only be construed as a seductive smile.

In his astonishment, Champ did not see the pot hole in front of him and the front wheel of his bike threw him off balance and into the ditch. A small feminine giggle only added to his embarrassed position in the ditch.

"Are you injured, sir?" She asked demurely from a safe distance.

"The only thing bruised is my ego," Champ replied sheepishly, as he realized his face was splattered with mud and his hands and knees there were covered with grass stains.

Because of the attire, he had assumed the old woman on this road earlier was Amish. Knowing about that culture, it surprised him that she would speak to an unfamiliar man.

"Pardon my intrusion onto your property Ma'am. I assume you live at the end of the lane in that beautiful little glen?"

Keeping her distance and speaking again very demurely, she answered. "Yes sir. I cannot remember when I did not live in this valley."

Champ thought about her answer for a few seconds and it made sense, if she had been born in that farm house he had seen. As the dusk grew more prominent, his mind was racing and his emotions toggling back and forth between fear and curiosity. Though peculiarly dressed, this woman was oddly alluring. His testosterone and common sense were having a significant quarrel.

If indeed Amish, Champ knew that if caught by her husband or brothers, it would be a serious issue for her...and for him as far as that goes. That thought gave the common sense a temporary upper hand in the argument going on within my body. He needed to get off her property and back to the 'safety' of his little cabin. However, now Mr. Testosterone appeared to take the lead. He could not leave without the answers to a few pressing and completely inappropriate questions.

"Do you have a family that runs the farm?" Champ asked.

"At one time, yes," was all she told him. Her response only added to his litany of questions.

"Well who runs the farm, now?"

"I do." Champ knew he was pressing his luck, but Mr. T. could not control himself at this point.

"I know this is none of my business, but are you Amish?"

She let out another soft giggle and surprised him with her response.

"No. Why do you ask?"

"I suppose because your attire is a little...a different from other women I've seen up here. And your mother or grandmother, or whoever it was that I saw earlier was dressed identical to you."

"My mother?"

"Well yes, not more than an hour ago I passed an elderly lady, with white hair, dressed exactly like you, and headed towards Gap Hill Road."

In response to his last statement, the woman said nothing and moved to continue her journey toward the valley where she lived. For some unexplainable reason, he did not want this exchange to end, so like a teenage boy, he blustered,

"My name is Champ Covington."

She stopped and turned slightly. "Yes…yes, I've heard about you. The author." She turned again to leave, but Champ could simply not let it alone.

"And what is your name?"

There was momentary silence. He wasn't sure she was going to answer him. Finally, she said softly, "Virginia." This time she did turn and walk away. Finally, common sense took a firm hold of him and he peddled toward home. Despite the growing darkness, his fear had minimized. Still, he knew he needed to be off Gap Hill Road before it was totally dark, so his peddling speed escalated.

Champ was nearly to the end of Tucker Farm Lane, when he said out loud to himself, "Virginia…That is a beautiful name." Suddenly, he heard a voice inside his head.

"My father named me after Virginia Dare. Many of us girls were named Virginia in those days."

Champ freaked and nearly spilled his bike again. Peddling now took on a frantic nature. He was terrified that a conversation would continue in his head and he did not want that. However, he found that he did want to encounter Virginia again. It appeared he had no control over this voice in his head.

"If you would like to see me again, you are welcome to come by and purchase some vegetables or a fresh jug of milk."

That was it! Champ decided he was going absolutely bonkers! By now he had reached his little cabin. It had never looked so inviting. Despite the fright of this situation, his curiosity could not help itself. Champ thought, "Well if I *am* really crazy, let's see what happens if I respond."

Champ said out loud to no one, "Great, I look forward to seeing you again sometime soon, Virginia,"

****

As he settled in his recliner in front of a warm fire, his mind was in a muddle. Never in his life had he engaged in such a bizarre conversation. Virginia had spoken in perfect English. Her accent sounded almost old English. He tried to remember. She definitely did not speak with the Southern drawl of other folks around here. He found it mystifying. When he commented about seeing her mother or grandmother, she looked shocked. His inquiry about the other woman he had seen on Tucker Farm Lane that day was met with silence. Despite the total coverage of clothing, he could see an unmistakable beauty beneath the bonnet. Mr. Testosterone won again. This woman would not leave his thoughts as he tried to relax and make sense of his day. One thing was for certain, he had to see her again.

Chapter 6

Lloyd Simmons had served eighteen years in prison for a murder he did not commit. The bullet that had killed the hunter was a clean shot. It had entered and exited the body and was never found. Lloyd's rifle had been fired, but it was from a week earlier. He had just never bothered cleaning the chamber.

The prosecution's entire case was based on circumstantial evidence. The trial had taken place in the Pickens County Courthouse and the jury was predominantly locals. He was definitely being railroaded and could not figure out why. With no family in the area, he had no one to speak for his character.

Lloyd spent much of his time in the prison library, studying the law in an attempt to clear himself. Finally, he connected with a young attorney in Greenville who, fresh out of law school, was eager to make a name for himself. He took on Lloyd's appeal pro bono, and given the circumstantial nature of the evidence, two decades later, a more enlightened judge overturned his conviction.

Lloyd had lost nearly twenty years of his young life behind those bars, but he had gained a valuable understanding of human nature. Upon return to his hometown, he kept mostly to himself, took up his old job at the logging company and resumed his passion for hunting. However, he never again went out hunting alone. The second thing he had gained in prison was a very unique nickname...Big Bongo.

On a Sunday afternoon in October several months after regaining his freedom, he decided to see if Bob's Place was still the best place to get a cheap beer. To his delight, he found several familiar friends from his earlier days. Nothing had changed up here. These guys were still sitting on the same rickety stools inside the bar, as they had 20 years prior. It was on this visit, that he met the famous author who needed a watch dog.

****

Around ten o'clock Monday morning Champ heard the unmistakable sound of an old truck pulling into his yard. He peered out the front window and was pleased to see Big Bongo emerge from behind the truck.

"Good morning," Champ greeted his new friend.

"And good morning to you, Mr. Famous Writer. I brought Sam over for a visit." Bongo retrieved a crate from the bed of his truck and set it down in front of Champ.

He bent down to look inside and Champ locked eyes with Sam for the first time. He was black with distinctive tan markings and large unruly ears. As Bongo opened the crate, Sam let out a long and mournful howl. Champ breathed a sigh of relief. If Sam howled that loud at night, nobody would bother him.

Bongo chuckled and told Champ that was Sam's greeting. Bongo hooked a leash to his collar and Sam lumbered out of the crate. He took a long look at Champ with the mournful eyes of a coonhound. He stretched, gave his flabby skin a good shaking and immediately laid down. Yup that was the nature of an old coonhound! Champ carefully approached the dog and gave him a scratch behind the ears. Sam almost purred. Champ decided this was going to be a perfect match. Once Sam sniffed Champ a few times, it appeared they would be fast friends.

Bongo had brought a couple of bowls for water and a twenty-five-pound bag of food.

Champ's training as a new dog owner, commenced. "Don't feed him much scraps. If you do give them to him, mix them with his food and add several cups of warm water. If you keep him in the house at night, he'll be your friend forever. But when he is outside, keep him on a leash. You don't want him wandering off in the woods and gettin' sideways of a bear."

The longer Big Bongo talked, the better Champ liked him. Intimidating? Absolutely! But genuine and friendly, too.

With the exception of his two decades in prison and his stint in the Army, he had lived in these hills all his life. Champ figured he must know most of the locals.

"Bongo." Champ hesitated for a couple of seconds, and then forged ahead. "I'm guessin' you probably know most of the folks living in the area, right?"

"I guess. Ya, I know most of them."

"Well the reason I'm asking is because I met a woman down on Tucker Farm Lane yesterday. In fact, there were two women. One was really old and the other one about my age. They were both a little strange. Do you know anything about them?"

Bongo took a long look at Champ and then responded in his soft voice.

"Mr. Champ, hasn't anyone told you not to wander off the main road? You told me you are writing a book about The Dark Corner, right?"

"That's right."

"Well, some of the folks up here aren't gonna be likin' you nosin' around in their business. Some of 'em still live like they did back in the twenties."

Champ interrupted him. "Tell me more."

"Well, during prohibition, this place didn't cotton to lawmen and didn't like outside folks pokin' around. It started when the government tried to collect taxes on our moonshine. We got our name as The Dark Corner 'cause locals moved deeper into the hills to avoid the revenuers. Guns were usually the deciding factor in who won a dispute. In fact, sometimes it still happens. I think that's what happened to me. I was jist in the wrong place at the wrong time. And so, I went to prison. You know I was spoofin' you when I said they never found the body. I was innocent of the murder they sent me up for and eventually, my case was overturned. You probably been real scared of me, haven't you?"

When Champ admitted that he had a little trepidation, Bongo let out a hearty laugh and apologized.

"O.K. I haven't answered your question 'bout the Tucker Farm and the two women. Were they by chance wearing long blue dresses and matching bonnets?"

"Yes, how did you know?"

"Well, it's what they always wear. Lots of folks up here know about that Tucker Farm. And really smart people don't bother 'em." When Champ looked inquisitive, Bongo continued.

"Been lots of stories over the years, about those women bein' witches."

"And what do you think of those stories, Bongo?"

"Not sure. It's just what the old folks 'round here say. One thing I can tell you Mr. Champ, is that when I was twelve, I walked down the Tucker Farm Lane just like you did yesterday. I had my varmint rifle with me and was lookin' to bring home supper. I was gettin' deep into the woods along the lane when I ran into this old woman, wearin' the same clothes you said she had on yesterday. This old lady didn't say a word. Just looked at me. I nodded, as I'd been taught and jist kept goin'. Not long after I bagged me a few squirrels and I was headed home, I ran into another woman. Only thing, this one was younger, and she was real purdy. Same thing. She didn't speak, just stared at me and kept walkin'. The reason I'm telling you this is cause over the years I've heard others tell the exact same story. It's spooky, Mr. Champ!

"And since you asked, I might as well go ahead and tell you. Doesn't seem to be no proof, but folks say that over the years, several young men went down Tucker Farm Lane tryin' to court the purdy one."

"What happened to them?" Champ asked, his curiosity now piqued.

"That's just it. They never been seen since. I know for a fact that the law went to the farmhouse couple of times and had a good look around. Nothin' ever came of it, though.

"Mr. Champ, you don't have to take my word for it, just ask a few of the ol' timers up at Bob's Place. But what I told you 'bout my experience when I was a boy...it's true."

Chapter 7

Monday night Champ had the best sleep he'd had since he rented the old cabin. He and Sam just hit it off. In addition to Sam's protective bark, Champ had purchased a Colt 45 and had it safely tucked in his desk drawer.

Tuesday morning Champ decided to take Sam with him into town. He didn't like putting Sam in the crate and it appeared Sam wasn't fond of it either. When Sam stood by the passenger side door and looked mournfully at Champ, he decided it was a mutual decision that Sam would ride shotgun. They road 20 miles west on Highway 11 heading for the big city of Salem. Sam loved to hang his head outside the window and let his big ears flap in the wind. Champ had never seen a dog look so happy.

Salem was a typical rural town. It boasted of two fire trucks, a five-member city council, and one leased police car that was being shared by two part-time officers. Luckily, Champ had been warned that Salem was a speed trap! The two main stores in town were a Dollar Store and an Ace Hardware. The Salem Methodist Church sat right in the middle of town up on a high bank where the road forked.

Today Champ's list included 25 pounds of dry food and a bear box for his trash. He also needed to find an electrician to wire the cabin for both front and back porch lights. He hated not being able to see outside after dark. He decided that the locals had gotten wind of his fear of the dark in the unfamiliar mountains. At a recent visit to Bob's Place, locals began telling him about super dense fogs that rose off the lake during the fall of the year. They called them 'Brave Eagle Fogs'. It had something to do with old Indian lore and Champ had heard just enough to have the hell spooked out of him. According to their colorful tales, you couldn't see your hand in front of your face.

Even with Sam and his new Colt 45, when blackness set in at night, Champ frequently wondered what had possessed him to settle in this long-forgotten land of corn liquor.

With errands completed, the pair stopped in Salem for a beer, but Champ made sure he could be home in the safe confines of his cabin before dark. He realized the stories about 'Brave Eagle Fog' were probably a fabrication, but in the present environment, he didn't want to take a chance. When he pulled up in front of the cabin, Champ noticed that the cord of firewood had been delivered and neatly stacked on his porch. Big Bongo had handled this for him and told Champ he could pay-up at Bob's Place over the weekend.

As October raced toward November, the daylight did not last long in these mountains. Champ hated that, as writing at night had lost its appeal. Even with Sam at his side, things that 'go bump in the night' permeated his imagination.

It was around ten-thirty that night when he heard a steady soft rain begin to pepper his tin roof. Still paranoid, he decided to forego the classical music he typically played when writing. Champ wanted to make sure he could hear any sound outside the cabin.

Despite all his concerns about the spooky events, Champ had no intention of abandoning his cabin for an apartment in Salem with noisy neighbors. After all, Champ decided, "I am a writer and fairly successful one at that. I need to conquer my silly fears and get my head into this novel about a moonshiner who actually still lives here in these Blue Ridge Mountains." He had done some research and was looking forward to the day when he would actually get to meet Tom Tatum, the legendary protagonist of his new book.

Champ had realized years ago that cooking for one was not any fun. But since there were no restaurants for miles around, he was forced to expand his culinary skills. That morning he put together ingredients for chili. He used way more ground beef than beans and probably twice the onion his recipe called for. His secret ingredient was a collection of spices that had been part of his mother's chili recipe. He put everything in a Dutch oven and placed coals around it in his fireplace, so it would simmer all day.

Much to his surprise, the chili turned out delicious! He made cornbread in the oven and polished off two bowls of the soup and half the bread. Against his better judgement, he even treated Sam to a little chili in his dog food. He was proud of his culinary success and with a sated stomach, he settled into his La-Z-Boy with the local paper. As he perused the few pages that interested him, he began to ponder how he might make contact with Tom Tatum. Bongo would be a good resource.

As the evening wore on, the temperature I his little cabin dipped below his comfort level and he reached for a blanket he kept handy for this type of evening. Rain on his tin roof was usually provided the same comfort as his chili and corn bread had been. However, this evening, even with Sam beside him snoring softly and the warming crackle of the fire, sleep eluded him. The constant drumming of rain drops only served to stimulate the thoughts rolling around in his head. Some of those thoughts involved Virginia, and Champ wondered how *she* might occupy herself on such rainy evenings.

Chapter 8

For four days the rain persisted, and fog obscured the mountain landscape. Although Champ could still hear the babbling brook beside his cabin, the fog was so thick that he could not see the stream when he stepped outside his door. Now, he truly understood cabin fever! Despite the fog, his need to get outside and talk with someone…anyone, was palpable. Sam must have felt the confinement as well, for when Champ grabbed his coat and opened the front door that old hound dog actually beat him to the truck. Off they went up into the hills towards Bob's Place. Even if only one person was sitting on a bar stool, that would be just fine with him. Besides cabin fever, Champ was also experiencing a bad case of loneliness. As he rounded the bend at the crest of the hill, bar looked closed, but then he spotted the small neon sign blinking its welcoming 'Open'. The younger of the two women who owned the hole-in-the-wall bar, was behind the counter. She smiled and stuck a cold beer in Champ's hand.

"Miss Mona, this is hospitality even beyond Chick-fil-A," Champ told her. He was so happy to have someone to talk to he was almost giddy.

"So, how's the famous writer?" She asked. "I see you and Sam have taken up company." Noticing the surprise on his face when he realized she knew Sam, she chuckled. "Honey, in these parts, everybody knows everybody. Human or canine."

"Mona, I'm bored out of my gourd, Champ complained. "I've never felt such isolation. The rain's not so bad but combine it with this murky fog and it's enough to make me pine for muggy Florida beaches. Writing is impossible! And my faithful companion here just sleeps his life away by the fire. I can't wait for this weather to break so I can get back to work on my novel."

"I hear your story is going to be about The Dark Corner, but what exactly are you writing about? This place is more boring than interesting. Sure, you will be able to sell the story once it's finished?"

"I'm fascinated with the moonshine business up here, Mona. I'd like to focus my story on a character I learned of on a History Channel episode. Evidently, he was a famous moonshiner. Name is Tom Tatum. You know him?"

"Are you serious? Everyone knows about Tom Tatum. You could write quite a story about that family. Funny, he was sittin' on that very stool you occupy, not an hour ago."

Champ was elated. "You've got to be kidding! I've been trying to figure out a way to get in touch with him. Do you know where he lives, and do you think he would talk to me?"

"Now don't let me confuse you, Champ. There was Big Tom Tatum and there is Little Tom Tatum. It was Little Tom that was in here. He's a regular in my bar. Big Tom's been gone about, oh, twenty or thirty years now. Most think that he was murdered, but nobody could prove it."

"I hate that I missed Little Tom, and I had no idea his father was dead. If you think Little Tom would be willing to talk with me about his father, where do you think I might find him...other than here of course?"

"Only other place I know of is 'The Barn'. But that's kind of a private place...locals only, you know."

With that piece of information, Mona ambled down the bar to greet another regular coming through the door. As Champ nursed his beer, he couldn't help wondering how he had missed the fact that Big Tom Tatum was dead. "So much for my thorough research," he thought. Well, it didn't mean an end to his story. He'd just have to find Little Tom and see if Little Tom would talk to him.

****

Listening is a keenly honed skill necessary for a good writer. Practicing that skill among the locals at Bob's Place, Champ learned more about 'The Barn', an underground gathering place frequented only on weekends between ten p.m. and the wee hours of the morning by locals...men only, to be specific.

With a few subtle inquires, he discovered that The Barn was tucked behind a dilapidated farmhouse about a mile off Highway 130. Patrons were mostly ridge runners who came down the mountain to sell their illegal shine and throw dice or play blackjack. He had heard that a generous shot of cold moonshine could be had for only a buck.

Champ had made inquiries with Big Bongo about Little Tom and whether he'd be welcome at this establishment. Bongo tilted his head sideways, thinking. Eventually he must have decided Champ would be welcome and told him that he'd let folks know Champ would be coming over for a sip of shine on Friday night.

Champ donned his oldest 'Dark Corner' clothes in an effort to blend and headed to The Barn. He sat in the darkness of his truck for a few minutes and observed. If local law enforcement knew about this place, they chose to leave it alone. Just standing in front of it, you'd never be able to tell there was a party going on inside. Shutters had been built to block out every bit of light and insulation had been added to the inside to contain the noise.

Champ slowly opened the door and ducked in as unobtrusively as possible. His attire allowed him to mostly fit in, as folks only glanced momentarily when he entered and then went back to their conversations. He made it to the bar and ordered a shot. Then Champ did what he always did when absorbing the environment for a story...he stood quietly at the makeshift bar and sipped his shine, observing the crowd and the games of chance. A thought popped into Champ's head, "I wished I were an artist, rather than an author. What a picture these mountain men would make." He decided that since he was truly an outsider, he would remain an observer, even if Little Tom Tatum did turn up.

At about eleven o'clock, a tall man with blond hair walked in. He shed a very wet yellow rain slicker and made his way to the bar, immediately ordering a couple of shots.

"Hey, kinda late for you ain't it?" An old man in the crowd called out.

"Na, the wife's gone visitin' and won't be home till tomorrow."

Another man sidled over to the tall blond and told him in a low voice, but one that Champ could still hear. "I heard that famous book writer guy was up at Bob's Place yesterday talkin' with Mona. He was lookin' to talk to Tom Tatum. Sounded like he didn't know yo' daddy was gone.

Told Mona he wanted to talk to you. Don't know, but I suspects you'll run into him up at Bob's."

"You say he's a book writer?" the tall man inquired.

"Uh huh. He actually rented that dilapidated Dexter cabin. Can yo' believe anyone would want to move up here to write a book?"

Chapter 9

Champ had accomplished what he wanted at The Barn and decided he'd leave that establishment to the locals. He quite liked the atmosphere at Bob's Place. It was an interesting combination of professionals escaping the city on weekends and colorful locals anytime, of day or night. So, the next weekend he and Sam headed back to his new favorite watering hole.

Champ had downed several beers when the rain and fog began to intensify, so as dusk gathered, Champ and Sam made a mad dash through the rain to the truck. That evening the fog was like pea soup, so the short eight miles down the curvy mountain road to his cabin took nearly an hour. It was dark when they reached his front yard. Champ parked as close to the cabin as possible. "That damn black fog," Champ said out loud. Sam let out a low grumble, as if validating Champ's complaint. As he prepared to make a mad dash to the door, the truck's headlights illuminated the porch. It was then that he noticed something was different. Sam contributed another low moan.

Champ had made a habit of turning on the floor lamp near his La-Z-Boy when he knew he'd be back after dark. Tonight, the cabin was dark. Maybe the bulb had burned out, but that seemed weird in itself, as he had just that week replaced the existing bulb with a brighter fifteen-year bulb.

As Camp and Sam dashed to the porch and unlocked the door, thunder and lightning permeated the hillside. Sam let out a low rumble as he entered the room in front of Champ. That dog hated thunder even more than Champ did. He followed his rumble with a higher pitched whimper, as if he was afraid. Just then a draft came down the chimney, causing the coals from the fire to glow brighter, illuminating the room. He stepped over to the floor lamp to test it. But before he even touched the lamp, it turned on and Champ had the shock of his life. Echoing Sam, he emitted a high-pitched squeal and stumbled backwards. Now Sam found his deep hound dog voice before Champ could recover and let out a long warning howl. Champ grabbed onto the table behind him in an attempt to regain his balance, but without success as he ended up on the floor.

In his La-Z-Boy, dressed in her blue frock and bonnet, sat Virginia. Champ was speechless. She slowly turned and looked down at him with those sparkling hazel eyes and that alluring smile he remembered from their first encounter.

"Sorry to startle you, Champ."

"But...but how, how did you get in here? I always, always lock the door and check the windows before I leave."

With a mischievous giggle she replied. "Guess we could just say I picked the lock, if that will satisfy you for the moment."

With that comment, her coyness did not infatuate Champ as much as it irritated him. She had broken into his home and she was making light of it.

"Nothing but the truth will satisfy me at this moment or any moment. Virginia, you nearly gave me a heart attack." He picked himself up off the floor and attempted to regain his dignity.

"If I had a phone in this cabin, I'd be calling the police right now." Just that thought made Champ feel extremely vulnerable in this isolated cabin. He walked over to check the door. It was locked from the inside. "How the hell did she unlock it and lock it again without a key? Shit, who was this woman?" he thought.

"Virginia, I have no clue how you broke into my house, but you owe me an explanation!"

"So what explanation do you think I owe you," she responded coyly.

"First, of all, how the hell did you get in here? Second, it has been pouring rain for hours and you are not wet, nor is my floor from the door to my chair you are occupying. Let's start there for explanations."

Just then, the infamous third step on Champ's front porch creaked. However, this time it was accompanied by a loud knock on the door and a brash voice hollered,

"Guess who I fetched to see you?"

Chapter 10

Although startling, at least the voice was one Champ was familiar with.

"Just a minute," he called back.

Wanting Virginia to be prepared to see Big Bongo, he turned to tell her who his visitor was. His La-Z-Boy sat empty. The fact that it was still rocking, was the only evidence that she had ever been there.

When Champ opened the front door, there stood his new friend Big Bongo, and a rather tall man who looked to be in his forties, with blue eyes and sandy colored hair. He was the man Champ had seen at The Barn.

With a great big grin on his large face, Bongo made the introductions.

"Mr. Champ, meet Little Tom Tatum."

Champ extended his hand and invited them both in out of the rain.

"I am so pleased to finally meet you, Mr. Tatum."

Tatum grinned and replied, "My daddy was Mr. Tatum. I'm just Little Tom, O.K?"

"Fine by me. And for both of you, I'm Champ, just Champ." Turning to Big Bongo when he said this to let him know he did not need to continue calling him 'Mr. Champ.'

Champ pulled up his only two other chairs from the kitchen table and placed them near the fire. He offered them a beer and for about an hour, they sat by the fire and chatted comfortably. Little Tom was well spoken and appeared to be more educated than many of the locals. His speech was not peppered with the standard Southern drawl.

"Little Tom, when I first moved up here, I was expecting to meet your father. After seeing the History Channel program on moonshine in The Dark Corner, I evidently didn't do my research well enough, for I had no idea he had passed," Champ told Tom.

"I'm sure by now, you've heard that I'm an author and moved here to write about The Dark Corner. Your father was well known during prohibition times, both within the area and now it seems beyond the Upstate of South Carolina. My intention was to see if I could make his acquaintance and learn firsthand about the moonshining business and the culture of the area. It has fascinated me for some time now."

"Champ, Bongo has told me all about meeting you. Since Bongo seems to think you are o.k., I'm sure my dad would have liked you as well." Little Tom grinned at Bongo and continued. "Big Tom Tatum had his faults, but he was a good father and husband. To me, that is a high endorsement for any man. His education only went through sixth grade, because at twelve years old, he had to work in the fields to help support the family. Those depression years were tough for everyone, but especially tough up here. Eventually, Big Tom joined others that were making better money with their moonshine.

"When my brother and I came along, Dad made sure that he did whatever it took to keep us in school. But that meant we had to do our part too. When we became teenagers, we had to help Dad with the distilling and bottling. His shine was considered some of the best liquor in these parts. He took pride in his work and supported our family for decades with his shine. But times changed and when he was murdered, my brother and I decided we needed to end the illegal business. Right after the funeral, we headed into the hills one last time and burned the still. Because Dad had insisted we get our education, it was possible for us to get jobs in Salem and help out our Mom."

Already, Champ could tell there was a great story here. Little Tom was both well-spoken and passionate. He knew it would take time for Little Tom to feel comfortable around him. Like many he had met up here, Champ was kept at arm's length at first. So, he decided to just let Tom talk instead of peppering him with questions. He was thankful that Big Bongo already thought enough of him to bring Little Tom to his cabin.

Champ noticed Little Tom staring into the fire, apparently deep in thought. He crushed his empty beer can and turned to Champ.

"Bongo tells me you met the blue ladies."

"Well, I didn't know that's what they were called until Bongo told me about them. A strange pair I must say. Have you met them, too?"

Little Tom nodded. After a few minutes he said, "When I was about seven, I remember Pa sharing stories he'd heard from my Grandpa about an old woman and young woman that could be seen walking on the back roads around here. Every time someone spotted them, the description of their attire was the same. They were attired in old-fashioned blue dresses and matching blue bonnets. As gossip and local lore usually does, the stories became exaggerated over time and young men were warned to keep their distance."

Champ was intrigued. "Interesting. That tracks with everything else I have heard. Have you ever seen them?"

"No, not personally, but I know Bongo told you about his encounter with them and I know a farmer down the way who has. Bongo tells me you have actually spoken to the young one. Is she as pretty as legend has it?"

Champ could not contain a grin that came over his face as he remembered the beautiful Virginia. "Yes. And in this case legend did not exaggerate. So, Tom, what do you think about these two ladies who seem to be quite the enigma?"

Tom smiled. "Well, I don't believe in ghosts. But from what I have heard, these two are rarely seen during the day...mostly at dusk. That alone is a little spooky."

The more they talked, the more Champ found himself thinking about Virginia's visit that very evening. He did not dare mention that to his two friends; for if he had, he was certain everybody in The Dark Corner would know by sundown tomorrow.

It was now past ten o'clock and the weather had only worsened. Thunder shook everything in Champ's cabin and when lightening lit up the sky, it only served to momentarily turn that hideous black fog, to an ashen grey. Then everything went black again. The deteriorating weather brought an end to their visit, and two new friends high-tailed it to Bongo's truck.

Champ had not counted the sequential days of rain, but it felt like at least ten days since he'd seen sunshine. His ability to write had also been sullied. Tomorrow, regardless of the weather, Champ was going for a bike ride...at least that was his resolve that night as he sat comfortably in front of his warm fireplace.

Chapter 11

As frequently happened, Champ spent the night dozing restlessly in his La-Z-Boy. He awoke just after dawn to find the rain had moved on and it was evident that the sun would soon make its appearance over the ridge. He made himself a cup of coffee and a piece of toast for his strawberry jam. When he smelled food, Sam appeared wagging his tail in hopes of his morning meal. Champ's restless sleep the previous night had been accompanied by thoughts of the beautiful young woman who had appeared mysteriously in the very chair where he had slept. He was certain it was the spirit of her presence in that chair that shaped his dreams.

When he raised the shade over the small kitchen window, he spotted the sun's first rays kissing the tops of the tall Poplar trees. Their leaves were now a brilliant yellow-orange and a gentle breeze was brushing them to the ground below. Champ's urge to get outside and ride intensified. Was it fed by a desire for exercise, or a drive to learn more about Virginia? Her audacious break-in and sudden disappearance perplexed him. He definitely needed to know more about this woman!

He could sense Sam had cabin fever as well, so he attached a long leash to his collar and out the driveway they went.

****

About three miles down Gap Hill Road towards Salem, he came to the now-familiar green sign for Tucker Farm Lane. Champ had to admit to himself, even in the daylight, that he was nervous. Here came Mr. Testosterone overtaking Champ's common sense again. He made the turn and peddled down the pot-holed drive. If he came face to face with Virginia, what would he say to her? What would she say to him? Could it be that the good ol' boys up here were playing some kind of trick on him? Common sense whispered in his ear that the legend of the blue ladies was obviously just a wild tale invented for the amusement of local folks. However, he knew he was not fantasizing about his encounters with both of them on this very path.

He peddled slowly down the road that led through the woods and beside the little creek. He did not want to push Sam, after all Sam was not a young dog and occasionally he wanted to exercise his coonhound traits by stopping and sniffing the air and the path before him.

As they neared the bend which hid the beautiful glen, the hairs on Sam's neck rose visibly, and he let out a long, low growl. And then the unanticipated happened.

Chapter 12

Up the road a piece Champ could see a large animal coming their way at a determined trot. His first impression was that it was a miniature horse. Sam knew otherwise. He came to a sudden stop which nearly jerked Champ off his bike. "Stupid me," thought Camp. Sam's rope was tied to the bike's handle bars. The hair along Sam's spine was at full attention, and a deep throated howl was coming from his gut as he dug his paws into the dirt to stand his ground.

The animal was now maybe a hundred yards away and closing fast. Suddenly, Champ realized this was not a small horse, but rather a giant dog with an immense coat of hair. That animal was at least four times the size of his Sam.

As the dog approached, he increased his speed and added an unfriendly snarl to his attack. It became obvious to Champ that he fully intended to protect his turf. He jumped off his bike and pulled Sam close to him. Sam and Champ realized at the same time that he was most likely the object of the oncoming attack and he scooted between Champ's legs for protection. He picked up a few large rocks in hopes of stopping the charging behemoth.

As the monster dog bared his teeth, Champ was certain he meant to tear one or both of them apart.

As the dog prepared to lunge, a woman's voice screamed from behind Champ.

"Brutus! Stop!"

Immediately the giant dog came to a sliding stop no more than three inches from Sam's nose. Poor Sam, was shivering and whimpering so loud, Champ was certain he had been injured.

He turned to see that it was Virginia who had issued the order. Champ too was shaking from the close call and yet still found himself speechless in her presence.

"Champ, I am so sorry about Brutus. No one ever comes on the farm that he is not familiar with. I probably need to put up some warning signs along the road. Are you OK?"

"Yes, I suppose so. I'm sure poor Sam thought he was about to be eaten. What breed is that monster dog?"

"Brutus is a Irish Wolf Hound. I'm told he is one of the largest breeds in the world."

After catching his breath, Champ decided now was as good a time as any to confront Virginia with his questions. He had her to himself on this road and it *was* broad daylight.

"Virginia...back to the explanations I was about to ask for last night when you so abruptly disappeared. How is it you come and go out of thin air? I just now came down the driveway and you were nowhere in sight. Exactly like last night!"

"Nothing mysterious Champ. I was over in the Rhododendron thicket picking herbs. You were occupied watching Brutus." She abruptly changed the subject. "So, Champ, what brings you all the way out here?"

"Isn't it obvious? As I just noted, you not only broke into my home, then you evaporated into thin air without so much as a goodbye or explanation of what you were doing there. I could not sleep thinking about you and what you wanted with me. So, I decided to come over and clear it up." Champ knew a change in tone was warranted if he wanted any answers, so he added, "Maybe over a cup of coffee?"

It worked, as Virginia responded. "Tell you what. When we get to the house, how about if I go in and get some cold apple cider? We can sit out under the big tree near the house and talk."

"Sounds good, and could you do something about Brutus? Poor Sam is still shaking, and he's an old dog. I don't want him to die of fright." She directed Brutus back to the house ahead of them.

When they arrived at the old farmhouse she left Champ and went inside. He carried his shivering hound dog over to a bench under the big oak and Sam took up his position under the table. He had so many questions about Virginia. He wanted to grill her but decided he might get more information if he played it cool and waited for her to take the lead. Perhaps some of the answers would naturally reveal themselves, given time. He wondered if perhaps her mother was inside, and it was not a good time for him to be introduced.

As Little Tom had noted, Virginia was wearing the same blue dress and bonnet. In a world where women changed clothes multiple times a day, this was very unusual.

Sam raised his ears a little and looked in the direction of the house. Virginia was coming out the door with a quart jar of cider and two glasses. Champ was expecting ice to be in the jar or the glasses, but soon discovered that the cider itself was very cold.

"I know what you are thinking Champ. No, I do not have ice, but I do have a cellar where I keep things cool."

"Isn't that the way people kept things cool in the old days?" Champ asked.

"My family has been using a deep cellar for hundreds of years. Never had an indoor refrigerator."

He was curious why she did not have a refrigerator, but it was not at the top of his list of questions, so he let it lie.

She sat across the table from him where her face caught the afternoon sun streaming through the remaining oak leaves. Despite all his questions and the untold number of warnings, Champ could not take his eyes off her. A tingle ran through his body that he had not felt for quite some time.

He decided to take a chance.

"Virginia, I've never seen you without your bonnet. How about taking it off, so I could look at you when we talk."

Champ could *feel* her blush more than actually see the color change on her skin. She took a little side look at him.

"I suppose. As a rule, I wear the bonnet to protect my face from the sun." With that, she untied the straps and gently let it slip off the back of her head. When it did, her beautiful auburn hair fell across her shoulders.

He was absolutely stunned by her beauty. She had the most exquisite face.

"Well, what do you think now that you have seen my full face...without makeup."

Champ's heart was pounding. He felt silly for his reaction.

"You are beautiful, Virginia. I'm surprised that men are not beating a path to your door." He was only partially teasing.

"Champ, have you forgotten my protector? Brutus?" she teased back.

They both had a good laugh about Brutus. At that reminder, he looked behind him to make sure Brutus was not close enough to attack if he made a false move.

Chapter 13

Champ's mind wandered as he sat at the table across from Virginia. As they talked he noticed she would occasionally steal glances at him, as if to figure out exactly what he wanted.

They made small talk as people normally did on a first date. But, this was not a date...far from it! Champ felt like he was looking into a piece of history. There was so much unknown with Virginia, but he couldn't quite put his finger on what had suddenly triggered this feeling. Perhaps he was letting Bongo's story get in the way of rational thinking.

In the middle of his contemplation, Virginia recalled that she had intended to bring out some cookies. She jumped up to get them. Champ had to admit, he had not been listening to what she was talking about.

As he waited for her to return, he took in the surroundings and tried to absorb everything he saw...and also the things he did not see.

First, he noticed that there was no car anywhere in sight. Neither was there anything that could be considered a garage. How did she and her mother get around, he wondered. A car could have been in the barn, but the barn door was padlocked and did not look like it had been opened for a very long time. Weeds grew high in front of the two doors. There was a well house near the back door and an outhouse about two hundred feet to the right of the house. Then Champ noticed there was no power line leading to the house. It was as if this place existed as it had two hundred years earlier. Now, the blue dress attire, was making sense, but the entire experience with Virginia and this farm, did not.

"Champ, are you in a daze?" He had not seen Virginia's approach.

"Merely deep in thought. It is very peaceful around here." He took a cookie and commented. "Very good. Did you bake the cookies?"

"My mother did," she replied.

"I don't see a car? How do you get to town?"

Because he had been letting Virginia take the lead, and had not peppered her with questions, this one was unexpected.

"It's not a problem. We walk and sometimes catch a ride."

Since there was no power running to the house, it followed that neither was there a phone line. This observation made her response ring rather untrue. But Champ did not pursue it further.

Although he had been married briefly and divorced only recently, outside that relationship, he had had very little experience with women. When their eyes met, it seemed as if she had a strange power over him. The logical side of his brain told him that was what women did to a man. He tried to resist the thought that he might be falling for this woman. He really didn't know her at all and so much was unexplained. Her speech was that of an educated woman, but an educated woman from another era. She was definitely secretive. A weird idea seeped into my mind: Had he stepped back in time when he rode his bike down her driveway? Several times he had been warned to steer clear of this place.

Where had the day gone? The sounds of Sam shuffling around under the table brought him back to the present and he realized that the sun was dropping behind the mountains. It was time to go. He had also noticed Virginia's mother peeking at him through the screen door. He bid his farewell and indicated as subtly as he could that he would like to see her again.

Virginia deciphered his intention and was less subtle. "Afternoons are best for a visit. When do you think you will be back, Champ?"

It was as if she had read his mind. He was startled but elated. "Would day after tomorrow work for you?" he asked.

Now she was feigning a more aloof demeanor. He was confused by her change in tone, but assumed it was due to her mother's presence.

"That would be very nice, she said. "I will perhaps see you then. And I will keep Brutus inside." She smiled, noticing his obvious discomfort at the mention of Brutus.

Sam was rested, and Champ wasn't sure who took the lead as they headed back home. All the way, he pondered a question he had not been able to ask Virginia. Why had she come to his cabin in the rain and how had she been able to get inside? Did she perhaps have a key to his house?

Chapter 14

As evening lengthened, his cabin grew chilly. Hot coals left from this morning's fire allowed him to get a good blaze going rather quickly. Although Virginia's cookies had been good, they had not sated his hunger and his left-over chili sounded mighty good.

Champ's original objective in moving to South Carolina had been to write a book about moonshiners and the effects of prohibition on these mountain families. He had found Little Tom Tatum, who seemed quite willing to share his father's story and the area's history. He had stumbled onto Bob's Place and Big Bongo. He certainly had enough material and definitely a perfect setting: a hundred-year-old cabin, deep in the shadows of The Dark Corner.

The only thing missing in his writer's toolkit was the internet. He did a good bit of writing based on what he had learned from local folks, but often he found he could not do without the internet for research, so he would trek to the local library in Salem.

Champ was frequently the only person in the library, other than the librarian. Either out of boredom, or out of curiosity, she was extremely helpful.

"Somewhere in the resource files, we have a local documentary on The Dark Corner. Would you like me to look for it? You could watch it on the computer."

Before Champ could even confirm or deny that he wanted to watch the documentary, she shuffled off to the archives and within minutes she handed him a DVD labeled *'The Dark Corner'*. It had been produced in Greenville, South Carolina, only fifty miles away, ironically by a company called Dark Corner Films.

Champ was ecstatic to find a local documentary on his chosen subject and he watched with relish. He had to admit that he hoped they would mention the legend of the blue ladies in the film, but regretfully they did not.

Champ had written dozens of books at this point in his career and knew that he had taken all the correct steps. He had uncovered significant information that would make for an interesting book, but for some reason, he found himself otherwise preoccupied and unable to fully immerse himself in the story of Big Tom Tatum and prohibition in The Dark Corner.

Virginia was now becoming a major distraction and Champ knew he was allowing it. He knew what was happening and no matter what he did, he could not get this woman out of my mind and Tom Tatum into it.

****

It was a beautiful December afternoon. Champ had taken a long bike ride up to Hog Back Mountain. His muscles had a thorough workout and he had exhausted all his remaining energy in the last few hundred yards up his driveway. As he approached his cabin, he saw a Dodge truck parked near the porch. He did not recognize the vehicle but did recognize the driver. The door opened, and Little Tom stepped out.

"Hey, what brings you up here?" Champ asked. Tom had a big grin on his face and replied.

"Well you said to drop by anytime, so here I am."

"Well it must be drink thirty somewhere in the world, so come on in and let's have a beer."

"Sounds good to me." Tom enthusiastically responded.

He threw a few logs on the coals and poked at them until a flame showed itself.

"I have beer and I've got a quart of blackberry shine that a friend of yours made. The choice is yours."

Tom's eyes opened wide and said. "Let me take a sip of the shine. I heard that Sammy Joe has really perfected it."

Champ had not yet tried the blackberry shine, so he was happy at Little Tom's choice.

One day several weeks earlier, while exploring an antique store in Walhalla, Champ had come across an old Kennedy rocker in pretty good condition. Remembering that he had been forced to offer Big Bongo and Little Tom rickety kitchen chairs when they had visited, he realized that he badly needed a guest chair. This evening when he was able to offer that comfortable rocker to little Tom, he was glad he had made the purchase.

Tom sank into the new guest chair and took a careful sip. "Man, this is the reason they call it White Lighting," Tom exclaimed. "Pour me a little more. I was out scouting game today and got rather chilled. Think I'll sit here and let both the fire and the shine warm me up. Damn this is smooth. I can feel it run clear to my butt."

Champ decided to pour another shot for myself as well and joined Tom by the fire.

"I was really glad to see you, Tom. Don't get much company up here."

The shine seemed to relax Little Tom. He was more talkative on this visit.

"How's your book coming?" Tom asked

"Slowly, very slowly. I've found a lot about the area and the local folks in general, but not much about your Dad. The only consistent fact is that he was considered somewhat of a legend in his time. No one wants to talk about the murder and not many want to talk about the moonshine business or the men that made it...back then or now. Guess it is still a little fresh?"

Little Tom nodded in concurrence. He took a slow sip and, still gazing into the fire he started:

"Well, I promised to tell you about my Dad some weeks back. But I have hesitated because even after all these years it is difficult to think about."

He seemed to change the subject. "I have checked out a couple of your other books, Champ, and you are certainly a first-class storyteller. So, if you have the time now, I'll tell you part of what I remember. We'll save the rest for another time." He said this as he held up his shot glass, indicating that blackberry moonshine might be the price I paid for his stories. That was perfectly fine with me.

"Now is good," I told him. "I have reached a stalemate or writer's block as they call it. Let me get a notepad."

This was exactly what Champ needed to take my mind off Virginia.

He sat back down with his pad but didn't say anything. He would let Tom take the lead and start whenever he was ready.

Little Tom leaned back in his rocker. He made several starts and it seemed that he was unsure just where he wanted to begin.

"One day back when I was nine and my brother Frank was fourteen, Dad piled us into his old pickup. He told us we were going to work with him and he would show us how he and Uncle Frank made their living. I thought we were going to see his farmer friends who sold hay. I had always thought that their business was purchasing hay from the farmers and selling it up in Ashville.

"Although it seemed like he had driven way back in the wilderness, we were actually not far from where a new lake was being built. We had been off the main dirt road for some time now, traveling over a rutted path. He stopped the truck near a small stream and looked us straight in the eye. We knew this look. It meant he had something very important to tell us. He started by warning us we must never, ever, tell anyone what we were about to see. If we did, it could get him sent to jail and our whole family could be in trouble. At nine years old, I was frightened but old enough to understand what he was saying and hoped my brother, who was mentally challenged, could comprehend the importance of this secret as well.

"We parked back in the woods off Highway 11. The little stream was a tributary of the Big Estatoee River. We crossed the river on a fallen log, then we followed a deer trail along the small stream through a dense thicket of Rhododendron. As we moved up through the hollow, I could smell a sweet smoke. Dad told us Uncle Frank was already up there and working. When we got near, I could see a large shiny tank with copper tubing at the top and a small fire underneath. Open wooden barrels stood close by and were filled with some kind of dirty-looking stuff that bubbled and gurgled. As Dad taught us the business, we learned that these bubbles were called 'snowballs'. A stack of gallon jugs created a wall on the upside of the clearing. Dad explained that he and Uncle Frank were making moonshine. When it was cooked and poured up in the jugs, they would deliver it to Ashville hidden under bales of hay. He told all this to my brother and me because now we were old enough to begin helping with the business.

"So that was my introduction to illegal moonshine. Looking back, it was a terrible way for a young man to start out, but it was the best my Daddy could do for his family at the time."

"How long ago was that, Tom?" Champ asked.

"Well, I'm now forty-nine, so about forty years ago"

"Tell me more about your Dad. I think I would have liked him."

"Well, I can tell you one story that may have been the beginning of the end for Dad.

"One hot summer afternoon the four of us were working the still, which was well hidden inside a Rhododendron Thicket. It was my brother who heard a noise down the trail. We stepped under a ledge where we were hidden but could observe from the shadows. We saw a large man coming up the trail using a walking staff for support. We watched him stoop to get a drink from the stream. He must have noticed that the water tasted tainted. We were close enough to see him make a face as he took his first swallow. He reached into the stream and picked up some of the grey-colored moss and looked around. He stood up and continued his ascent up the trail. When he neared where were hiding, my dad slipped out behind him. The man had stopped by a tree to catch his breath, and that was when my dad cocked his rifle and asked the man what he was doing.

"The man raised his hands in the air and without turning around, insisted that he was not the law, but only out for a walk in the warm weather. Then he added that he collected Indian artifacts, which was the purpose of his walk up this hill. I remember my Dad telling him there weren't any Indian artifacts to be found on a mountainside. He informed the intruder that anybody who was serious about collecting Indian artifacts, knew that! The man then asked my dad if he was going to shoot him." Little Tom chuckled at this memory. "My Dad said, 'I'm a thinkin' 'bout it.'

"The man really had a sense of humor. Even as a teenager, I could tell that. He told my dad that since he was obviously NOT going to shoot him, he'd like to drop his arms and turn around. I think my Dad appreciated the man's sense of humor as well. He allowed the man to turn around but threatened him, that if he ever told anyone about this place he had just discovered, he could expect to be shot. The big man had a smile on his face and introduced himself as Stone Mountain Kennedy.

"Kennedy further endeared himself to my Dad by adding that he had never tasted moonshine and would love to try a sip. My dad glanced over at Uncle Frank and asked him to pour up a little out of his reserve barrel. Frank handed Stone Kennedy a small jar of the shine. He took a few sips and I remember him licking his lips, commenting on how smooth it was. He and my Dad and Frank sat on some logs near the still for some time. I remember wishing the man would go away, as my brother and I had been instructed to stay hidden under the ledge. My Dad really took a liking to the man. He actually invited him to our house to show Kennedy his collection of arrowheads. Finally, Stone Mountain said his goodbyes and headed back down the trail."

"Two questions," Champ interrupted. "First, just what is a reserve barrel?"

Tom explained, "In the old days, moonshiners would take a small barrel and fill it with what they felt was the very best brew. They submerged it in the stream to keep it cool. It was significant that Dad offered it to Stone, as only special friends were given drinks from this barrel."

"Very interesting, Tom." Champ's curiosity was piqued. "My second question is about Stone Mountain Kennedy. I noticed you called him by his first and middle name. Did you get to know him personally? And was he the one responsible for your Dad's murder?"

Tom hesitated a minute before answering. Champ could tell this was not easy for him. "Yes, I did get to know Stone Kennedy, but he did not murder my dad. He really liked my Dad, but as I told you earlier, it was his connection with Stone that I believe *got* him killed. I'll tell you a little more, but the whole story about Stone Mountain Kennedy will have to be for another time. It is quite a tale!"

Little Tom paused and took another sip of the blackberry shine and before continuing.

"About two weeks later Kennedy came up to our house. I watched the two men sharing their Indian arrowhead and pottery shard collections and it was amazing to watch these two, with such different backgrounds, forge a friendship.

"Not long after that, I overheard my dad make a call to Kennedy, who lived in Greenville. I didn't hear the whole conversation, but it was about the new lake that was being built by the regional power company. There was an issue, and he wanted Kennedy to meet him up near the lake bed late that night. It had something to do with an old Indian burial ground that would be destroyed when the lake bed was flooded; and an Indian talisman. Evidently my Dad and Kennedy stole that talisman from the site that night."

Champ could tell Tom was having increasing trouble reliving this story about his father's death, so he suggested that they call it a night and get together again soon. Tom actually looked relieved. He patted Sam on the head as he got up to leave. Sam didn't even open his eyes. He just twitched and moaned as if in the middle of a doggy dream.

Chapter 15

Champ walked Little Tom to the door and stood on the porch, watching him drive away. It was early December and the night was very chilly, so he quickly headed back to the comfort of his fireplace. He hadn't eaten that evening and knew he needed something in his stomach to mitigate the effect of the blackberry shots. Champ had become quite fond of some of the Southern delicacies, and one of his favorites was fried bologna sandwiches. So, he fixed one and grabbed a beer to wash it down with. Then he settled into his recliner to ponder what Little Tom had shared. Finally, his head was back in the story about Big Tom Tatum. He would quickly need to resume writing so that he could effectively incorporate the material he had just been given.

As he relaxed in his La-Z-Boy, enjoying his sandwich, he thought he caught a slight movement of the Kennedy rocker. It was almost imperceptible. When he turned his head, of course no one was actually sitting in the chair. He figured if he looked directly at the chair, he would realize that it was the result of too many shots this evening; but the chair continued its slight rocking motion.

Champ stepped over to the rocker and placed his hand on it to stop the rocking. When he was satisfied that the rocker was not moving he sat back down and started thinking again about his novel. He had almost dozed off, but slightly spooked by the motion of the rocker, he wanted to make sure he wasn't going nuts before he let himself fall completely asleep. When he again glanced at the rocker it was moving! What on earth was causing this? Was there a vibration somewhere in the house that he could not discern? He put his index finger on the arm of the chair to see if he could feel any kind of vibration but felt none. After the chair stopped this time, it did not move again that night. He knew that because he slept fitfully in his recliner, keeping one eye open most of the night.

Since moving into this cabin, a number of things had spooked him. As he laid back in his recliner trying to fall asleep, he was thinking about Virginia. Purposely, he had not seen her now in three weeks and he was hoping that he had not disappointed her by delaying his return. He had needed some space and a major refocus. Maybe he would wait another week before heading back up to Tucker Farm Lane again.

The next evening, Champ prepared a more sophisticated dinner of macaroni and cheese, again with a beer. He watched the chair as he ate and again he detected the Kennedy rocker moving. It was still daylight, but that did not stop the creepy feeling that slithered up his spine. He decided to just sit there and watch the chair to see how long the phenomenon would continue. As he watched, his mind wandered back to the night a couple of months ago when he had come home to find Virginia sitting in his La-Z-Boy. He knew it sounded crazy, but he wondered if it was possible that Virginia was sitting in that rocker right now. So, he called out. "Virginia, are you sitting in that chair?" Just saying it out loud made him feel both stupid and eccentric. Little did he know that was only the beginning. When the rocker suddenly stopped, he couldn't decide if he should bolt for the door to get out of this crazy environment or if he really wanted to see Virginia sitting in his living room again.

"Virginia! Stop these antics and show yourself. This is getting tedious."

Part of him figured it had to be Virginia. After all, what else could it be? Another part of him never expected anything to happen, and believed it had to be a seismic phenomenon. The chair began to move again. Now he could not take his eyes off the rocker. A figure began take shape in the chair. He had never seen a ghost, but he was certain that is what he was experiencing. His stomach turned summersaults and he hoped the macaroni and beer wasn't going to wind up on the floor.

Virginia turned towards him with that mischievous smile on her face.

"Champ, please don't be frightened of me. I am harmless. And I am lonely. You have not returned to visit me as you had promised. I had to come see if something was wrong."

Champ's mouth felt extremely dry, and he was not sure he could form words.

"You know, you could have knocked at the door...like a normal person. That being said, I've felt from the first day I met you that something was different about you. But invading my home twice, uninvited, disturbs me! You really do owe me an explanation. I don't believe in ghosts, but I don't know any other description of your behavior. You can either explain yourself now, or you can get out and stay out." Champ really didn't feel quite as angry with her as his words sounded, but he was confused and, he had to admit, a little frightened.

"Not sure where you want me to begin, Champ?"

He decided to start out small, before he asked her to explain the whole 'ghost' thing. "Well how about telling me how old you are and where you are from?"

Virginia looked as if she had pity for him. "I was born in 1751 somewhere in the Colony of Virginia. I guess if you did the math, that would make me about two hundred-sixty-seven years old."

If Champ had been speechless before, now he was dumbfounded and questioning his sanity. Perhaps he was in the middle of a vivid dream. The look on Virginia's face told him she knew what was going through my mind. She did not continue, but smiled tenderly and allowed him to soak this in.

"Champ, I realize this must be confusing. My story is a long one and I won't be able to explain everything tonight. I will tell you that I had a very happy childhood and an early marriage that was not so happy. My family moved from Virginia when I was about ten and settled here. We farmed this area when the Cherokee were still living nearby. I'm not sure I can explain the phenomenon I live with, but when I died at the age of 40 from a fever, it appears my spirit lived on and since that time, I have always looked as I do now. I am sure you have heard the gossip about me. I did marry two more men in the past two hundred years. I realize that that is incomprehensible to you and I don't even know how to understand it myself. I do remember that the last two marriages were happy ones. Despite that, this perpetual existence is really a curse.

"The older woman that you have seen on the path and in my home is my mother. She lives with the same curse I do, but she died at an older age and has remained at that age for a very, very long time."

What Virginia was telling Champ was so incomprehensible that he worried he was delusional. "You were married three times you say? That couldn't have comprised the entire two hundred-sixty-seven years!" Champ didn't know whether he was angrier or more curious.

"I know it is just one more unfathomable detail, but the entire two hundred-sixty-seven years are not clear in my mind. The best I can explain it even to myself, is that I think my spirit periodically returns to the grave. Perhaps seeing the cemetery on the farm would be helpful to as you try to understand me. If you come to my house again, we can walk up to the old cemetery. If you have time next week, I will try to answer more of your questions."

Still in a daze over all this, Champ needed desperately to do something…anything; so, he walked over to the fireplace and stared into the flames, trying to make sense of Virginia. He put a couple more logs on the fire and turned to ask Virginia about her husbands. He wanted to know if they had known about her vaporous activities. But she was gone!

Chapter 16

Three weeks went by and Champ did not return to Virginia's home. He could neither make myself ride to Tucker Farm Lane, nor could he concentrate on anything else. His thoughts frequently revisited their recent encounter. In the evenings, he would sit in his La-Z-Boy and stare at the Kennedy rocker, willing it to begin rocking. He began to think he should move back to Florida before these incidents with Virginia drove him certifiably insane.

Despite Little Tom's unbelievable story about his Dad's death, writing the story of Big Tom Tatum had lost all of its intrigue and the process of extracting words from his brain had become all but impossible. Champ decided that talking to Little Tom again might pull him out of his writer's block. So, on Saturday afternoon, Champ took Sam and drove up to Bob's Place hoping to find Tom there. He was in luck. He caught sight of Little Tom leaning on the counter inside the bar talking with friends. When he spotted Champ, he waved him over to join the group. It was a pleasant afternoon, and just what Champ had needed. Little Tom's friends had been welcoming and he enjoyed the banter about the lumber business, hunting and even a little local gossip. Before he headed home,

Tom agreed to stop by the next evening and continue the story about his Dad.

* * * * *

True to his word, Tom arrived just as the sun was setting and they resumed their places in the La-Z-Boy and the Kennedy rocker...this time with a few beers instead of the shine.

After Champ had been as patient as he could with small talk, he brought the topic around to Big Tom, hoping Little Tom would not feel pressured.

"Feel up to finishing the story about the call your Dad made to Stone Mountain Kennedy?" Champ prodded.

"I'll try," agreed Tom. "It is a tough story for me and it doesn't get any easier to tell as time goes by." Tom hesitated for a very long minute and as Champ was about to tell him that he did not need to do this, he began.

"Remember I told you that my Dad and Kennedy took a precious talismans from Indian burial ground. It was made of onyx and in the shape of a bear.

"My Great Uncle Jess, who'd lived in these parts for nearly a hundred years, swore that the talisman was cursed and anyone who touched it would die a violent death.

"It was shortly after the talismans was taken, that my Dad disappeared. His truck was found about a week later in the woods near the lake that the power company was building. But there was no evidence of my Dad.

"About two weeks after my dad disappeared, I realized I needed to get away for a bit. It had been a difficult time for my family and everyone was leaning on me for decisions and support. I lit out very early in the morning to hunt from my deer stand. It was dark when I climbed into the tree. As the sun came up over the mountains, I could begin to see movement, and thought I had spotted a deer, so tensed and prepared my rifle in anticipation. I waited for a clearer shot, but it turned out to be a couple of crows circling low to the ground on the sandbar not far from me. Soon five or six more dove from the tree tops and landed in the same area. They were noisier than normal for that time of day and began fussing and fluttering as if competing for something to eat. I became curious and left my tree stand to see what they were fighting over. As I approached the sandbar, the stench of rotted meat permeated the air. Where crows were concerned, that was not unusual, but this morning they were fighting over the remains of a human skull.

"Crows or scavenging animals had done a thorough job of eating most of the flesh off the skull. Clinging to the skull were a few spots of skin and some patches of hair.

The eyeballs were gone, and worms were finishing off the eye sockets. Even the lips and ears had been eaten away."

"Oh God!" Champ exclaimed, feeling nauseated. The look on Champ's face must have told Tom his description had been disturbingly vivid.

"I'm sorry Champ. I probably should have warned you. I know this is repulsive. When I saw it, I became nauseated too and I didn't then even know whose skull it was. I did know that I needed to get home and call the sheriff. As I turned to head back to my truck, I noticed a spear stuck in the sand with a scalp attached at the top.

"Champ, I literally ran the entire mile back up the hill to my truck. I think I knew that it was my Dad, but I did not want to believe it."

Tom paused. I could see how hard it was for him to relive the story. The writer in me knew that this would make a very exciting book, but I found myself torn between wanting to hear what happened next and feeling compassion for Tom.

"Tom, I'm so sorry. If I had known what I was asking you to relive, I'd never have asked. Let's stop." Champ apologized.

"No, I promised to tell you and It is easier to finish tonight than have to get into it again another night," Little Tom admitted, so he continued.

"Despite the fact that we did not like the law around our property because of the moonshine business, that morning I did call the sheriff.

"A whole team of forensics people ended up at the sandbar. Turns out the body was buried in the sand in a sitting position. They speculated that sand had been packed so tightly around his chest it impeded breathing and that was the cause of death. Of course, the crows and the scalping may have also played a part."

Champ interrupted Little Tom to ask. "So, what about the Indian spear with the scalp? That is just creepy in this day and age."

He responded, evasively. "A story for another time, Champ. Back to the story about my Dad's death. As I feared, they soon confirmed, that the body was my Pa. As I told you before, it was right after the funeral, that my brother and I headed up to the mountains and destroyed the still."

That appeared to be the end of Little Tom's story-telling that night. He sat quietly for a long time and just stared into the fire. There were still a lot questions running through Champ's head, but Little Tom had made it clear they would have to wait for another time.

Chapter 17

There wasn't a moment that went by that Champ wasn't torn between the story he came to write and his obsession with Virginia. Over the course of a couple of weeks it dawned on Champ that the story he should be writing about was the so-called legend of the blue ladies. But he was now too far into the Tom Tatum novel, so the blue ladies would have to wait. This was the source of his writer's block. He was supposed to be writing a novel about a moonshiner, but his mind was preoccupied with the mysterious Virginia and the paranormal.

On Christmas Eve, he left Sam by the fire, grabbed his keys and headed down the road to Virginia's house. There had been an abnormal amount of snow this year, according to talk at the hardware store. When he turned onto Tucker Farm Lane, it was obvious that no cars or trucks had been in or out of that road. The snow was still about six inches deep. For the first time he also noticed there was no mail box.

Champ had been into Seneca the week before the snow and bought some gifts for Big Bongo, Little Tom, Virginia and her mother. He had delivered all but the last two.

He parked in front of the house and waited for Brutus's appearance. He did not materialize and neither did Virginia. So, he grabbed his Christmas gift bag and made his way up the steps. It was nearly dark, and no lights were to be seen in the front windows. He remembered then that this house had no electricity. He saw no sign of Christmas decorations. Cautiously, he knocked on the front door. A dim glow appeared momentarily in the window to his right. A voice called out "Who is it?" He responded, "it's Champ Covington."

The door opened and there stood Virginia with a kerosene lamp in her hand. She was beautiful with the lamp glow reflecting on her face.

"Oh Champ, I did not think I would ever see you again. Please come in."

He stepped into a very dark, cold house. The only light was the one Virginia held. He knew there was no electricity, but he thought there should at least be a fire for heat, if not light of some kind.

Virginia either saw the confusion on his face or sensed his observations. She answered his questions, before he even asked them. "Neither my mother nor I need heat or light. However, I can see that the lack of light and warmth are bothering you. There are some logs in the fireplace left from a fire some time back. Let me get some paper and we will soon have a warm fire for you."

Champ knew the answer to his next question, but he asked anyway.

"Is your mother here? I was hoping to meet her and give her a small gift."

"I'm sorry Champ, but she is upstairs and does not accept guests."

He said nothing, but irony struck him: Why would a ghost need to go to bed?

Soon they had a nice fire going as the wood was extremely dry. No telling how many years it had sat by that fireplace. Virginia retrieved another lamp, which gave the room a very cozy and romantic atmosphere. There was not a couch, but there were two comfortable rockers with wicker bottoms that sagged like they had seen many years of use.

Champ set his Christmas bag down on the old hand-braided rug. Virginia asked, "Is it Christmas?"

"How could you not know that?" he asked with incredulity.

"Well when you think about it, time doesn't mean a lot to me. It's been at least a century since I recognized holidays. And I see mistletoe attached to the gift on top. It appears, you are a romantic, Champ."

He couldn't figure out how to answer, so he didn't. Virginia looked at him with a tender smile.

She asked in a teasing tone, "Champ, I thought you agreed to come visit me again shortly after I was last at your cabin. It has been a long time since that night. Did you forget about me?"

"Well, to be honest, I have not been able to get you off my mind since I met you last fall. You have been very disruptive to my concentration. Normally, when writing a book, I would be well along into my story by this time, but now I cannot seem to focus."

"And why is that my fault?" she asked coyly.

"Virginia, by your own admission, you are not a normal mortal woman. I have never met anyone like you, and only read stories about characters with paranormal powers."

"There are books about people like me?"

"Yes, but they are works of fiction or at least I assumed they were."

Now it was my time to change the subject. "So, tell me Virginia, you are obviously interested in me. I would like to know why."

"Well since we are being honest, I am lonely. And Champ, you are a very nice-looking man and not married."

"Under the guise of honesty, I too am enamored with you," I admitted. "But to be honest, you and I are very, very different."

"Different how?"

"Well, Isn't that obvious? I was born in the later part of the last century and if I'm fortunate will live into my eighties. That will be in this twenty-first century. You have already lived over two and a half centuries. When I die, I hope to go to heaven. You will just go to sleep in your grave and by some magical power, wake up sometime in the distant future to live again among normal humans. That in itself is a major difference. Then there is the issue of being able to appear and disappear. And I believe, to also read minds. Isn't that enough difference? I'm sure it is obvious I'm attracted to you, both because you are a phenomenon and a very beautiful woman."

"Phenomenon? What does that mean?"

"It means you are extraordinary and with remarkable abilities."

"I believe those are compliments, so thank you. I do not recognize some of your words but get the gist of their meaning. Your vocabulary is two centuries more advanced than mine, so please forgive my limited knowledge."

Again, he changed the subject. With where this conversation was headed, he couldn't help myself. "I don't believe I have ever touched you. Are you as you appear...real flesh and bone?"

"Yes, don't be silly. Of course, I'm living in a body just like you."

With that she reached over and lightly touched his face with her fingers and a tingling sensation ran throughout his body. He knew what these feelings were, but he never thought one could get aroused by a ghost!

Their exploration of intimate feelings ended when Virginia stood and began poking the fire. He removed her gift from the bag and when she returned to her chair, he handed her a small gift box.

"Oh, this is so beautifully wrapped, I hate to even open it." However, she removed the ribbon and paper and Champ was delighted to see a look of genuine pleasure light up her face.

"Oh Champ, you are so thoughtful. I really needed a new hair brush and comb. They are so elegantly decorated."

"I'm glad you like it. Please give your mother this gift in the morning. By the way where is Brutus?"

"He is most likely lying on the rug next to my mother." I was relieved, and hope he stayed there.

Sleet began to pepper the tin roof. Champ observed Virginia glance toward the stairs. Not sure if this meant she was worried about her mother waking or Brutus again protecting his territory. Either way, he took it as a signal to leave before he got stuck in her rutted driveway.

He bid her farewell and paused, hoping it was not obvious that a goodnight kiss was on his mind. He considered making the move, but in the end, decided against it. If she was responsive, he would be even more tormented in the days to come.

"Champ, I hate for you to leave, but I do understand. If the weather clears and you can make your way back down my road next week, I have an idea I'd like to share with you about an adventure we could take together."

What a titillating suggestion she dropped, just as he was about to leave. He started to ask her about it, but she quickly opened the door for him and said, "Goodnight Champ."

****

Champ's imagination went wild for a whole five days. Finally, he had a plan. He headed to the Salem Dollar Store and selected several healthy snacks and a couple of fruit drinks. He put the food in a basket that he had found at a yard sale and headed for Virginia's farm. This time he drove the pick-up, just in case Brutus was on patrol. Champ pulled up in front of the house and got his basket of treats. He left Sam inside for safekeeping. He had just headed toward front door when Virginia stepped out.

"What a pleasant surprise. It is good to see you again so soon," Virginia greeted him.

Champ held out the basket to her. "I brought a few treats. I'm hoping your offer of a walk to the cemetery is convenient today?"

"Of course. I have a perfect place up in the hollow where we can enjoy this unseasonably warm afternoon."

Being a man, he took this as an invitation of an intimate nature. Virginia went back in the house and retrieved an old quilt for their picnic. He wondered what her mother was thinking about this exploit. The fact that she was centuries old and they did not have a not proper escort, must seem improper to her. Champ didn't care!

As they started up the hill, he heard a familiar howl and suddenly remembered he had left Sam in the truck. Champ asked Virginia if he might bring Sam with them.

That triggered concern about Brutus's whereabouts. He looked around and his panic brought a small chuckle from Virginia. She assured him that Brutus would remain in the house with her mother and would not be a problem.

His emotions were running wildly out of control and again he wondered if he was falling for this mysterious woman. He had heard that opposites attract. Champ was a city boy and Virginia lived like a country girl, but the differences were much greater than that. Champ was curious why none of her marriages had produced children. Perhaps ghosts can't conceive. That thought made him smile.

It was an unseasonably warm day for the end of December and the snows of previous weeks had long since melted. She led him along a narrow path that followed the stream. Sam loved this outing and dutifully followed their lead. Virginia stopped in a secluded area encircled by Mountain Laurel. A melodious waterfall fed the small stream. The entire setting was picturesque, even in the middle of winter. Water from the falls tumbled over large boulders and splashed into a pool below.

Virginia spread the old quilt out on a bed of leaves, sat down and began to unpack the basket. Champ was delighted to see that she had removed her bonnet and allowed her hair to cascade over her shoulders. For the first time, he could appreciate the fullness of her breasts.

He could not take my eyes off her and had a strong desire to touch her.

Sam appeared as enamored with this place as Champ was. He sniffed the air and wandered in search of scents he wanted to chase. Luckily, he found nothing to follow, and tiring of the hunt, he settled down beside Champ on the blanket.

Their conversation was light for a while, but he needed to take advantage of this time alone with her, so he initiated line of questioning that he hoped would not be objectionable. Champ desperately hoped that they would get to the proposition she had dangled in front of him the last time we were together.

"Virginia, do you read? You seem to be well educated."

"Yes, I do read books. Mostly about the world as it is today, so that I understand the culture I am living in. Politics do not interest me at all. I believe the last great President we had was Mr. Lincoln."

I chuckled and teased her. "You almost sound like you knew him."

"No, I never had the pleasure of meeting him, but I could have."

Champ thought this was an odd thing to say. It sounded like she was living during Lincoln's time. Then he realized, of course she was alive at that time. A little shiver came over him as he remembered what Bongo had told him. Three men had tried to gain favor with the young blue lady and had never been seen again.

"Virginia, I need to be totally honest with you."

"Please do," she responded with a quizzical cock of her head.

"I am very enamored with you and yet I barely know you. From the first time I saw you on the lane...there was something I felt. I know you live an unusual existence, but as beautiful as you are, I'm sure you hear that a lot."

"You are right about one observation, I do live an unusual existence. But you are wrong about the other. Because I live in such solitude, I do not encounter men who are interested in me. It is one of the greatest regrets I have." She paused as if to add to her comments and then it appeared she changed her mind.

Champ took that as closure to their picnic and suggested, "It will be dark soon, so I propose we start back toward the house."

Chapter 18

Over three weeks went by before he saw Virginia again. He was nearly forty years old and could not remember experiencing feelings this profound. Much of the time, he felt childish…giddy. Then at times it was like someone slapped him across the face. His thoughts were mature, and he seriously pondered what life would be like with a woman who did not drive a car; did not have a phone or electric lights or even indoor bathroom facilities. He could not comprehend what day-to-day life would be like. His best guess was that it would be like living in the past. In those rational moments, he knew he did not want to forego all the modern conveniences that 2018 held.

Another recurring concern was her inconsistent behavior. She had dangled an adventure in front of him the evening he brought her a Christmas present. Then she avoided telling him about it. Her behavior was at once seductive and aloof. It reminded him of a fly fisherman that would float a caddisfly in front of a trout and then jerk it away to entice the fish into taking a fatal bite of the imposter caddisfly. Like the trout, he could not help myself.

On the fourth week, Champ again arrived unannounced at Virginia's doorstep. When one's intended paramour has neither a phone or a mailbox, it is difficult to give advance notice of your arrival. He traveled in his pickup as a safeguard against Brutus and again brought a lunch to Virginia's house. This time he thought it prudent to leave Sam at home.

Unlike Champ, Spring was giving advance notice of its arrival. Pink cherry blossoms and white dogwoods were peeking from dormant branches. They headed back towards the waterfall and repeated their first visit there with the blanket, food and circuitous conversation. The afternoon flew by and he thought Virginia was bringing it to a close when she suggested they put the food back in the basket. He made every effort to hide his disappointment, for he still did not know any more about her illusive invitation. But she surprised him.

"Champ, let's put the rest of the food back in the basket. I want to take you a little further up the path to show you something very special."

They came to the edge of the Mountain Laurel that surrounded their small clearing. At this point, he lost the path. However, Virginia knew it well, and she put out her hand for him to follow her. His heart skipped several beats. Soon the Laurel ended, and a denser thicket of Rhododendron took its place. In his research he had learned that Rhododendrons were known as 'jewels of the mountains'. The ones they were making their way through were mature. Some of the trunks were almost as large as the pine trees. Like a shroud, they hovered over the two, blocking the sun's rays.

They climbed for nearly a half an hour and emerged from the 'jewels' onto a level plateau. Once Champ's eyes again became accustomed to the bright sunlight, he spotted a cluster of very old grave stones, with the surrounding grounds very neatly manicured. It was obvious that someone maintained this little cemetery. Even though the dates on the markers went back a hundred or more years, Champ could easily read the inscriptions on the granite tombstones.

Virginia stopped short of entering the cemetery and allowed him to inspect the stones. He counted six. Three of them were virtually identical and placed in a perfect row. The other three were all different.

He knew Virginia had a specific purpose for bringing him to this very private cemetery, so he took his time and read each stone.

James Thornhill 1816-1871
Civil War

William McGregor 1768-1829
American Patriot

Manning VanHouser 1763-1793
American Revolution

Joseph Dare
1692 - 1751
Father & Husband
Descendant of Ananis Dare

Linda Dare
1695 – 1763
Wife and Mother

Virginia Jennie Dare
1751 – 1791

Chapter 19

Virginia Jennie Dare, 1751 to 1791. That was *her* grave! A thought struck Champ upside the head like a boxer's blow. The beautiful and mysterious Virginia; her very own grave, sequestered deep in these Blue Ridge Mountains; and a yet to be identified adventure for the two of them. This was fodder for a best-selling novel, if he ever saw one! The creative possibilities were unfathomable...and yet, this was *not* fiction. He was actually living these unbelievable events.

As he studied each grave marker, he watched for a hint of what had motivated Virginia to bring him up here today. As he had these thoughts, he felt her strong presence standing behind him. It was another instance where he truly believed she read his mind. He read the marker that bore her name. Then I read it again. This Virginia Dare dies in 1791 or two hundred and twenty-seven years ago. And 'his Virginia' told him she was two hundred sixty-seven years old. *This was her grave!*

Champ turned to look at her and his expression must have revealed his next question.

"Virginia, are you related to everyone in this cemetery?"

"Yes, I am...all except the last one."

"You mean Virginia Jennie Dare?" He was not sure he wanted to hear her answer.

"That is the one I mean. Champ," she hesitated "I'm not who you think I am. I'm not even what you think I am."

Although he suspected what she was about to tell him, he was not sure he wanted her to reveal it, as he feared it might change his life. Virginia looked straight into his eyes and confessed:

"Virginia Jennie Dare, lying in that grave, is me."

****

Champ wanted to respond, but the truth was, he did not know what to say. He had suspected she was a ghost, but he was not sure he wanted to admit he believed in such fantasies. However, she had appeared and disappeared without explanation. And he was certain she could read his thoughts.

Virginia surmised his difficulty and continued, "Champ, my life and death have become a long and complicated story. You write fictional novels which require a great deal of imagination and I think you will need every bit of your imaginative powers to digest my story.

"I was born in Virginia in 1751 and moved to the farmhouse when I was ten years old. As I already told you, I died in 1791. I cannot tell you how I became what I am now. What I can tell you, dear Champ, is that I am falling in love with you."

This confession Champ did not expect! His first reaction was to turn and run as fast as he could to his truck and not stop till he was back in Florida. In retrospect, it is exactly what he should have done! However, his writer's curiosity, his growing emotional connection to this woman and his common sense, were in serious conflict. Part of him was tingling at her confession of affection. She had said she loved him!

At long last, he was able to verbalize a few of his thoughts.

"O.K. first let me address what my rational mind can get a handle around. Just who are the other people in this cemetery?"

"Joseph and Linda were my mother and father." She hesitated for a long time before continuing.

"The three men, James, William and Manning were my three husbands."

His instinct to cut and run came back, with more intensity this time. And yet he did not move. He was still standing in front of the head stones, so he studied the names and the years they had lived. Without a calculator it was a little more than he could do in his head. He could see that VanHouser was born in 1736 and McGregor in 1768; but the third one, James Thornhill wasn't born until 1816…twenty-five years after she'd died!

All this was just too much to comprehend. Champ made some excuse to head back down to the truck and bid his farewell with as much civility as he could muster. All he wanted was to 'get the hell out of dodge'.

Chapter 20

Champ had never known what it felt like to be tormented, until the week after Virginia made those two unbelievable confessions. Every day he reaffirmed his conscious decision to NOT to see Virginia again…maybe ever! But his heart was telling him one thing, and his brain, quite another. Of course, everyone knows that the emotions involved in love and the rationale of common sense have nothing in common. He decided what he needed was the company of male companions, so he nodded toward the truck and Sam took the hint. Off they went toward Bob's place.

It was Saturday afternoon and the usual suspects were gathering for a few beers at Bob's Place. By this time, Champ was one of the 'usual suspects'. A voice at the end of the bar called out, "Bongo, it's yo' turn to buy a round." Bongo obliged. When he spotted Champ, they made their way to a few stumps outside, away from the Harley crowd and also away from the local crowd. Champ needed to confide in someone and Bongo had become his best friend over the past couple of months. So he spilled his guts and got exactly what he expected from Bongo.

"Oh Champ!" Bongo bemoaned when Champ had finished sharing some of the details of his 'dates' with Virginia. "Now, I'm not anyone who needs to be handing out advice, but from what you're telling me, you're falling for this lady. You have been warned, multiple times, man. This woman can lead to big trouble and I hate to see it happen. I told you months back, that a couple of other guys got themselves involved with her and they have flat out disappeared. And that's a fact!" Bongo could really deliver a lecture and Champ knew that he needed his friend's level head. Still, the heart wanted, what the heart wanted.

"Bongo, I hear what you are saying, and I appreciate your concern, but she intrigues me, for several reasons. She is obviously beautiful, but also has some unique, let's say, abilities that I want to explore. For right now, I am going to continue seeing her." Bongo raised his eyebrows and shook his head obviously realizing he was not going to deter Champ.

He chose not to tell Bongo what he knew about Virginia. He knew from Bongo's raised eyebrows what he thought Champ meant when I said Virginia had 'unique abilities that he wanted to explore'. Champ figured he'd just let his friend's imagination run wild.

Chapter 21

As the locals had come to accept Champ, they were now more comfortable talking about Big Tom Tatum. All that led to additional material for his novel. So, it should have been a slam dunk for Champ to write this story...but it wasn't! Champ thought if he could get the rest of the story of Big Tom Tatum's death, it might be the impetus he needed.

This time when they met, he was invited to Little Tom's house. Champ took that as a sign that he had been accepted. They had a pleasant evening and when he realized it was past time to head home, it was nearly midnight. As he pulled onto the road that led to his little cabin, he could see smoke coming from his chimney. By this time, Champ knew it meant he had unexpected company. He opened the front door, and standing in front of the fire, was the beautiful Virginia.

"Well hello!" Champ said, with obvious pleasure at finding her in his home.

"I do hope my presence does not inconvenience you," she said.

"Not at all," he laughed. "I have become accustomed to your sudden appearances. It no longer frightens me. But please, do me a favor. Let me know when you are leaving. It is unnerving to turn around and find that you have just vaporized."

She nodded her head but made no further commitment.

"I was hoping we could have a little chat; that is if you have time," she requested.

"Well, my only chore is to get Sam some supper. Let me take care of that and we can visit."

For an old dog, Sam was always hungry, so at the mention of his name, his tail began to wag. Although Virginia had Brutus, Champ was surprised that she had no affection for Sam. On several of her visits he approached her but must have sensed either her lack of interest or he was nervous about her ghostliness and backed off. Evidently, they came to a mutual agreement, as Sam did not come looking for affection and she made no overture to pet him. Champ thought that was unusual.

After Sam was fed, Champ settled in his La-Z-Boy. Virginia chose in the Kennedy rocker.

Champ opened the conversation, as he was still anxious to hear about her Christmas eve proposition. "OK, what's on your mind Miss Virginia?"

"Champ, I know you are up here to write about the moonshiners and Big Tom Tatum. But as a writer, my guess is you are always on the lookout for a good story. Am I right?"

"Spot on," I confirmed.

Virginia looked quizzical, not understanding the phrase, so he clarified. "I meant, yes you are right."

Once she understood his meaning, she proceeded.

"Do you remember my mention of an adventure you and I could take together?"

He did not want to reveal his obsessive curiosity about this teaser she had thrown at him on Christmas Eve, so he merely replied, "Yes I seem to remember you saying something about an adventure."

"Well, I believe this journey would present an opportunity for you to write a novel that could really make you famous".

Champ was eager to finally hear what she had in mind, but needed a few minutes to settle his nerves, so he deflected.

"Well, Virginia, as you noted previously, you do not read fiction, so you are obviously not aware, but I am already a very famous author. However, that being said, you do have my attention. Please go on." That braggadocios statement stabilized his nerves, and he felt he was ready to hear what she had to say.

"This would be quite an unusual adventure for you, so I recommend you think about it for a day or so and then give me your answer."

"You've teased me long enough with this proposition, Virginia. It's time you shared the details."

My slight tone of angst went unnoticed by Virginia. She left a very long moment of silence hang in the air as she stared into the fire. Finally, she turned to face me.

"What I'm asking you to consider is a trip back to a time when America was very young."

That was the bombshell. Champ needed to be sure he understood her proposal. "You mean like a time machine?"

"I'm not sure I know what that is, but it I am proposing time travel back several hundred years to Williamsburg, Virginia."

He did not mean to sound flippant, but it sure came out that way. "Like snapping your fingers, we suddenly find ourselves in colonial Williamsburg two hundred years ago?"

"It's not quite that simple, Champ." Virginia said patiently. "But the results are the same."

Over the course of his acquaintance with Virginia, he had come to terms with the ghost concept, but time travel...was a whole new notion he was not prepared for. Still feeling that he needed to protect himself, he preserved his flippant tone.

"O.K., so I go on this trip through time with you; can I assume you will bring me back to the present?"

"Yes, Champ." Although her tone still sounded patient, it was slightly less friendly.

"Anytime I want to?" he pursued.

Champ should have picked up on the fact that she never directly answered his question, but rapidly moved on to explain in more detail.

"I can take you to places that I'm familiar with. Places where I lived at the time. You will be in a unique position to actually experience history. As an author, would that not give you a very distinct advantage?"

He ignored her question and chided, "Sounds like Alice in Wonderland, to me. And by the way, just how long would we be gone?"

"When we get back, time here will be virtually the same. You will hardly know that you had been gone," she said.

Again, he should have picked up on the deflection. Instead, being a very pragmatic person, he was focused on getting more information.

"I don't mean to sound like a smart ass, but to even consider this crazy idea, I need more details. So, do I just hold your hand and poof, we arrive wherever?"

"It will be fast, but not in a puff of smoke as you suggest."

He continued his drill. "O.K. more details...what do I need to prepare? What do I need to take with me?"

"I would suggest that you go to a bank and convert your current currency into old gold coins. Gold is acceptable almost anywhere and would look normal to people living in the past."

"Although that makes sense, Virginia, I can't just walk into a bank and get old gold coins. That would need to be done through an antique coin dealer. It will take some time." As much as he was in the dark about the past, he realized she was just as ignorant about the present.

"You can leave all your possessions as they are now and when you return, even your food will be as fresh as you left it."

"What about Sam?" Champ asked.

"Sam cannot accompany us. I suggest you leave your animal with a friend until you return."

"But what about luggage?" he persisted. Hard to imagine traveling without it.

"I suggest that you wear old jeans and a long-sleeved shirt. You will want to dress for what the weather is, so it would be prudent to wait until after we arrive to get more clothing. A gold coin will go a long way in purchasing what you need. Do not wear a hat. The hats of those times are very different than what you wear today. There are no hats around here like you will see in Williamsburg."

Now he was getting curious. "Won't I stand out and look different?"

"That's why it's important for you to purchase new clothes as soon as we reach our destination, so that you will fit in."

"Where will we stay?"

"You will most likely stay at a boarding house and I will stay at my home."

Now this is where he thought he needed to put his foot down.

"What do you mean your home? Your home is here at the end of Tucker Farm Lane."

"That of course is true. It is my home, but in the 1750's when I was a child I lived with my parents in Williamsburg and the family retained the Virginia home for many years. In the year we will arrive, my family still owned the home in Williamsburg."

"What about your mother. Will she go with us?"

"No. She will stay here and wait for me to return."

My final question was 'when do we leave'?

"I suggest we leave Saturday afternoon. The streets in Williamsburg will be busy and we will not be noticed. We will arrive in the year 1791."

Virginia continued, "Champ, if you decide to make this journey with me, be at my home on Saturday afternoon at three o'clock and we will begin our journey."

"Virginia, *if* I decide to make this crazy journey, Saturday is not possible. If I need to take gold coins, it may take me a week to get them. I don't know much about what I will need, but I will not travel without money."

"My apologies," Virginia replied. "I had not thought about that. Very well then, we will make it the following Saturday. You do not need to come to the house to let me know your decision. I will know it, the minute you decide. I am leaving now, Champ."

Good to her word, she did let him know she was about to vaporize. He was actually ready for her to leave. He needed time to think about this outrageous proposal.

If he were to go, he had work to do. He needed to see if Big Bongo could take care of Sam and also keep an eye on his cabin. Provided he could source gold coins, he could be ready a week from Saturday. Now that he had all the pragmatic decisions made, the harder decision would take some time.

Chapter 22

Champ was parked in front of the bank in Salem at ten o'clock Monday morning when they opened. He figured they would be the best source for a local coin dealer. The teller drew a blank when Champ told her what he needed. Luckily, the bank manager was a coin collector and he steered Champ to a reputable local dealer.

He found Samuel Joseph at a little shop next to Paesano's Italian, Champ's new favorite restaurant in South Carolina. He used the bank manager as a reference and stunned the man by informing him that he needed two thousand dollars in gold coins, they needed to be dated earlier than 1790, and he needed them in seven days. Champ also stipulated that they be in small denominations. The coin dealer's eyes grew wide and he opened his mouth as if to ask a question, then immediately closed it, evidently thinking better of it.

To reinforce what Champ assumed he was thinking, he merely added, "If you don't want to know the answer, it is best not to ask." The dealer nodded and set his fingers flying at his computer in search of the coins. After a few minutes, he told Champ that he could get them, but that he would pay a premium. Champ agreed, and the dealer asked for Champ's phone number, so that he could call when they arrived. This amount was more than Virginia had suggested. But he decided he needed a cushion in case things in 1791 went 'south' as they say. It would be his security blanket.

****

Big Bongo and Champ had formed a strong bond. Champ knew he was someone he could trust with anything...including his valued Sam. He needed to tell someone about his plans. Monday afternoon he called Bongo, who immediately sensed the urgency in Champ's voice. He told Champ he was working, but suggested they meet at Bob's Place around five.

Champ arrived at Bob's Place a little early. He bought six beers and headed back to his truck, thinking that would be a more private place to discuss this crazy adventure. He didn't need any big ears listening in.

Bongo saw his truck as he came around the curve in his yellow jeep. He pulled up beside the truck and Champ motioned for him to climb in, holding up a beer to let him know he had refreshments.

"This must be very important," Bongo said with a rare smile. "I'd bet my next paycheck that this has to do with that blue lady."

Champ laughed nervously and nodded. "Yes, this has to do with Virginia Dare."

"So that's her name? In all the stories I've heard about the blue ladies, I never heard a name before."

Champ knew if he didn't get the story out quickly, he might change his mind about telling Bongo the whole tale.

"OK, I'm going to tell you my story. Bongo, I trust you or we wouldn't be here. This conversation must remain between you and me. Is that understood? Once you hear it, you'll understand why."

"Got it…just between the two of us."

"You already know I have seen Virginia on a number of occasions. What I never admitted is that you were correct when you said she was strange. On several occasions she has appeared in my cabin unannounced. The first time she appeared in my cabin before I got home, and the door was locked."

"Really, how'd she get in?"

"This is what you are not going to believe, Bongo. She just appears out of thin air. I know that sounds weird, but I swear on my mother's grave, it has happened several times."

Bongo's face darkened. "You tellin' me she's a ghost?"

"I'll tell you right up front, I've never believed in ghosts. But there is no other way to define what she can do."

"Like in the movies, can you see right through her?"

"No, no, nothing like that. Just like you and me. She eats and is flesh and blood; but she has lived in the past and has the ability to transfer her spirit or whatever you call it, back and forth in time."

"Like a time machine?"

"Something like that, but I don't know exactly how she does it. O.K., here is what will really blow your mind! She was born in 1751 and died in 1791 at the age of forty. She even took me up to the family cemetery and showed me her grave."

"Her grave? Champ, even though I'd heard tales for years, you are freaking me out!"

"I know...I know. I saw her grave, graves of her mother and father. And... graves of three men she claims were her husbands."

"Champ, if I didn't know you as well as I think I do, I'd say you're full o' shit."

Champ realized how all this must sound to Bongo, so he handed him another beer and forged ahead before Bongo could bolt from the truck.

"O.K. so here's the rest of the story."

Bongo interrupted incredulously, "You mean there is more?"

"Yes, just listen. Virginia approached me last week and said that she had an opportunity for a story that would really get my attention. According to her, she can take me back with her in time and I could actually live in colonial America and experience history firsthand. No writer gets that opportunity!"

"Assuming she can do this time travel, and I doubt she can, are you going to do it?"

"Bongo, I thought long and hard about this and my curiosity is just wired! So, the short answer is, yes. We leave next Saturday."

Champ gave Bongo all the details about the gold coins and how he would dress. He also asked if Bongo would look after his cabin and take Sam home with him. Bongo agreed but told Champ he was still not convinced he would follow through with the 'stupid plan'.

Just in case things went wrong, Champ told Bongo where the old cemetery was and asked him to check it for a headstone with Champ's name on it if he didn't return in a couple of months. That request Bongo would **not** agree to.

"I'll do about anything for you Champ, 'cept that. You will never catch me on that property, much less at that gravesite." Bongo went on to tell Champ how ill-advised he thought it was to place himself in danger, as he put it.

"What are you going to do if you get into some kind of trouble back two hundred years ago and can't get back?"

"I don't have an answer for that. Guess I'll send for you to come rescue me." They both laughed at that non-possibility.

Chapter 23

On Wednesday Champ drove to the coin dealer to pick up his gold coins. They were much heavier than he had imagined. He realized that he could not just walk around with a bunch of coins in his pocket. If he got robbed, then he *would* be stuck.

He stopped in the Dollar Store on the way home and bought a small sewing kit. He thought his plan was brilliant. He would sew the coins into his pants and take them out as needed.

The Salem Library was on the way out of town, so Champ stopped to do a little research. He wanted to find photos of how men dressed two hundred years ago. He did not want to dress like a plantation owner, but Virginia had told him to look like a farmer. He could see right away that he did not own any clothes that looked remotely like the ill-fitting shirts or pants from the 1700's. What he needed were some worn out baggy pants and shirts. The only place to look for what he needed was at the Goodwill store in Seneca. It did not take him long to realize that clothes in the Goodwill looked newer than what he needed. His only other option was an antique store. He asked around and found one that had a collection of colonial era clothes and hats. He found what he needed, including a winter coat; and he headed to his cabin.

He tried on the clothes and could not believe how full the pants were. The legs felt big enough for two people. That was perfect for his sewing plan with the coins. The shirt looked large enough for a man Bongo's size. But research at the Library had revealed that this was the style of the day, two hundred years ago. Champ decided that wearing two pairs of underwear would be a good idea, for obvious reasons.

Big Bongo came by on Friday and picked up Sam. He still was not on board with Champ's exploit, but he wished him good luck and again advised him to change his mind. "You may never be able to come back. Think about that, Champ."

As Bongo drove off with old Sam in the back of his truck, Champ wondered if he would ever see either of them again.

****

He was nervous as he drove toward Virginia's house on Saturday. She had told him that he could not carry anything but the clothes on his back. So, if he was allowed to carry the gold coins, why not also carry something else. He found a couple of things in his belongings from that general time period and added them to his travel possessions. He had located a pocket-sized Bible that his grandmother had given him as a small boy, and an old Prince Albert tobacco can that fit in his shirt pocket. In it he put some Imodium, Aleve and cold pills. He also took his reading glasses.

Upon arriving at Virginia's place, Champ noticed that the barn door was open. Virginia had suggested that he leave his truck in the barn along with the keys. Her point was that he should have nothing modern on his person...such as car keys. She would not know about the medicine, but no one else would know either.

When she came out of the house she took a look at him and let out hardy laugh.

"What's so funny?"

"It's just the way you look in those old baggy clothes."

"Do you think I will fit in?"

"Oh yes, you will definitely fit in! They will think you are a country bumpkin."

"Well, I followed your instructions on dress," Champ snapped back. Her chiding smile made him feel very self-conscious. Despite the fact that she had on the same blue print dress, she looked much more sophisticated than he did.

Virginia walked back to house to say goodbye to her mother. When she returned she looked at him and asked,

"Ready for our big adventure, Champ?"

"Admittedly, I'm more than a little anxious. Actually, I'm very apprehensive."

"You know you don't have to go. I will understand if you change your mind, even now."

"If I think about it anymore, I probably will change my mind. Let's go."

Chapter 24

It was mid-afternoon by the time they entered the small clearing where the old tomb stones stood like sentinels, watching over the two remaining Dare women. As he looked around, he noted that not one leaf remained on the towering oak trees above us.

He was extremely nervous. Virginia moved over next to him and took his hand. He was certain she was reading his mind. She told him to remain calm and assured him that he would not feel any discomfort during their travels. It was the first time she had held his hand and it had its intended affect.

"Champ, you will feel is as if you are in some wonderful dream."

Her words almost sounded like the description of a soul's trip to heaven. He remained quiet as Virginia had directed and tried not to misconstrue her words about the travel experience.

She kept hold of his hand as she walked toward her own headstone. He did not know what would come next and did not like this. He had no choice but to follow her.

"Come with me, Champ. I want you to lay down beside me."

She laid down on top of her own grave and pulled him down towards her. "Oh God, what had I done?" Champ thought. He wanted more than anything in the world to bolt. But she tightened her grip on his hand to the point he fell to the ground next to her. Fear gripped every inch of his body.

"Champ, it is very important that you keep a firm grip on my hand so that we arrive together."

She began an incantation, soft at first and growing louder. He could not tell if she was speaking English or another language. However, he sensed more than heard her ask for a safe journey. It was almost like a prayer.

Champ felt as if the grave was opening up and swallowing them. He had his eyes scrunched so tight that his lids ached. Virginia instructed him that under no circumstance was he to open his eyes until she told him to open them. "Damn straight," Champ thought. There was no way he wanted to see what was about to happen.

"Champ, this journey may seem short, but you will never forget it." He didn't care if he remembered it. He just wanted to live through it.

It must have been stress that brought a humorous thought to Champ's head. Perhaps Bongo and Little Tom would come jumping out of the woods right then and laugh at his naivete'.

But that did not happen. He felt his body move. He heard a crow calling out from nearby and thought of Little Tom's story about the crows.

He felt a tremble under his back. At first the vibration was soft, but soon it began to rumble. He sensed that he was levitating. His body felt numb and he had the urge to pee. "Lord please don't let me do that," Champ thought.

His breathing became heavy and he lost his ability to hear. It was like he was in a sound chamber. Since they were moving through space and time, he assumed he would hear wind, but there was no sound. Apparently, however, his sense of smell had not left him. Fragrances he had never experienced wafted past him. Then he began feel the sensation of tumbling head over heel with increasing speed.

Champ still had a firm grip on Virginia's hand but this time it was him that was squeezing hard. He wondered if she could hear his thoughts.

"Yes, I can hear you my love," came Virginia's words in Champ's head.

"Can I open my eyes now", Champ thought.

"Oh, please do. I don't want you to miss this part of the experience."

Gingerly, Champ opened one eye just a little. When they left Salem, the sky had been a bright winter blue. Now it was jet black. Billions of stars twinkled endlessly, and the moon looked close enough to touch.

Cautiously, he turned his face towards Virginia. She was looking at him with a broad smile on her face. He sensed speed, yet he had nothing to gage it by.

Virginia squeezed his hand and told him to again close his eyes tightly as the band of light that separated the centuries would be blindingly bright. He did as instructed, but this time, not from fear. Even with his eyes closed, the golden light penetrated his eye lids.

Virginia whispered that they would soon arrive at their destination. Champ could not describe the euphoria, or the relief he felt. Now he believed he would live through this experience to arrive in colonial Williamsburg, Virginia in the year 1791.

Chapter 25

Virginia squeezed his hand, probably to make sure she had his attention. She again whispered to Champ.

"When we arrive, we will probably be standing somewhere near the center of town. It is Saturday afternoon, so the street will be crowded with people, horses and wagons. You are dressed like a farmer who is in town to sell his merchandise. Most people will be dressed in their best clothes. I will land somewhere on the street, but we will not hold hands or be standing next to each other. I am dressed like a lady of means and would not be seen in the company of a farmer. It is my fault that you are dressed like a farmer, but I don't know where you would have gotten gentleman's clothes. I will walk ahead of you and stop briefly in front of a store where you can secure more appropriate clothing. Make your purchases and I will wait for you in the center of town near a large statue. The street will be North Henry Street.

"You have your gold coins, so you can secure what you need. I suggest you tell the shopkeeper that you have come to town to buy new Sunday clothes."

Champ absorbed her instructions and thought it ironic that he had been a lawyer, and a celebrated author and now he was posing as a farm hand. He had no clue what farmers talked about, so hoped the shopkeeper did not try to make small talk, about crops, livestock, etc.

****

"Champ, it is critical that you act normal."

"Act normal? Champ thought. "There is absolutely nothing normal about traveling two hundred years through time...with a ghost!"

Suddenly, he felt that his feet were on solid ground. His legs had become weak during their trip, which made him feel a little off balance. He realized he had just stumbled.

Virginia had already separated herself from him and was taking steps into a crowd of people. Champ looked down at his feet. His left foot was almost ankle deep in a pot hole filled with muddy water and his right foot was solidly planted in fresh horse shit. Later, he would learn that he had touched down smack dab at the intersection of Lafayette and North Henry Streets...the hub of colonial Williamsburg in 1791.

When his ears regained normalcy, he I was startled to hear several people hollering at him from somewhere in the crowd.

"Hey, country bumpkin! Move out of the way! You are in the middle of the street, blocking the funeral procession for Mr. William Holt. Are you daft?"

He could see a number of horses and fancy carriages heading directly toward him. Long lines of people were standing on both sides of the street to pay their respects to this aristocratic landowner.

Champ lowered his head to avoid making eye contact with anyone and hustled to the wooden boardwalk. Immediately he became aware of how shabby his clothes looked compared to the gentry of Williamsburg. He truly felt out of place. Still with his head down, he made his way to the rear of the throng where he looked for Virginia.

He could hear the horseshoes clicking on the cobblestones as the procession headed in his direction. Curiosity made him linger to observe an eighteenth-century funeral.

In front a small band played soft, mournful music. They were followed by four oversized carriages, varnished black and trimmed in gold. Pulling each carriage was a team of four white horses adorned with tall black tassels mounted on each side of their heads. Driving the team with four in hand, were two men in tall grey hats and black suits. Champ guessed that inside was the family. The fifth carriage carried the coffin. This carriage was being drawn by six regal black horses, adorned with a tall black feather plume. A funeral in London would not have been any finer than this. The white hearse, which was extremely ornate, carried a carved wooden casket protected by glass panels. The coffin was draped with a massive spray of red roses. The single driver with six in hand was dressed totally in white. Just behind the hearse, led by an attendant, was William Holt's horse. It was a beautiful chestnut gelding. The empty saddle atop the horse held holster and pistols. "What a magnificent sight!" thought Champ.

Following the funeral procession walked pall bearers, representatives from the Masonic order and perhaps a hundred or more mourners. This was his introduction to Williamsburg Virginia.

He started walking in the direction Virginia had gone and picked up on the fact that townspeople either stared at his clothing or ignored him all together. He wondered how he had failed to seriously research the clothes of the day. He had managed to humiliate myself.

To avoid bumping into people, he followed the funeral procession, leaving enough distance that it was not assumed he was part of that gathering. He headed towards Virginia. As he neared the statue, he spotted her seated on a bench in the open sunlight. Regardless of the century, she was a beautiful woman.

Champ saw another place across from her to sit. It was close enough for her to speak to him and far enough away that people would not assume they were together. She pointed to a general store across the street whose sign read: Dry Goods and Grocery.

In a loud whisper he said. "I have a twenty-dollar gold coin. Do you think that will be enough to get new pants and a shirt?"

She chuckled, "Yes, and with change back to you."

He stood up and made his way across the busy street to the establishment. A man in a white apron stood near the door. When he felt Champ was about it enter the store he spoke.

"Best of the afternoon to you."

"And good afternoon to you sir." Champ responded.

"Anything I can help you with today?"

"If you carry clothes, I may be interested."

"We mostly sell gentlemen's clothes. But if you are looking for work clothes, there is a feed store just down the block that carries a good selection."

"Actually, I'm looking to buy some Sunday clothes."

"Well in that case, you may find something in our dry goods to your liking. Mr. DeWitt will be happy to help you."

Champ's eyes had to adjust as he made his way to the back of the store. There were no lights. Then it dawned on him that the lightbulb had not yet been invented. From behind a sackcloth curtain, he noticed a short man heading in his direction. He assumed this was Mr. DeWitt.

"Yes Sir, anything I can help you with?"

"I need to get me some Sunday clothes."

A little condescendingly he responded. "Well, I think that most of what we carry would be considered Sunday clothes."

He was studying Champ's attire with interest.

"I've been selling clothes for a long time; I suppose you would know where yours were made?"

I decided to patronize him and said. "I'm not sure, but maybe the label says where they were made."

DeWitt continued. "I ner' seen a label in farmers clothes. Labels mostly come in expensive clothes displaying the tailor's name. The reason I'm asking is because I've never seen clothes made quite like yours."

"Not sure what you mean, sir." Champ responded

"I suppose it's the cut of the breeches and your shirt has a collar design I'm not familiar with."

Champ reached to the back of his shirt collar and pulled it down.

"Take a look and see it says where it was made?"

DeWitt pulled the label down for trying to read what it said.

"My Lord, this says 'Made in China'. I ner' seen anything made in China. I mean the stitching is so fine and exact. How did they do this?" Mr. DeWitt pondered. It would be fifty years from this time before Elias Howe invented the first American sewing machine.

Of course, Champ had no answer for that and realized he might have made his second mistake of the day.

"Mr. DeWitt, can you give me an idea what trousers, a shirt, waistcoat and shoes would cost me?"

The little man brightened at the prospect of a sale of this magnitude. "Well let's just step over here to my work desk and I will make you a list of the price of each piece. I will warn you though that you might not be able to afford this extravagance on a farmer's wage."

DeWitt smiled condescendingly. Champ knew the salesman was thinking that he most likely did not have enough to pay for even a pair of trousers.

Champ recognized his desk as an antique standing desk from the seventeenth century. It stood about chest high. Of course, in 1791 it was not yet an antique! Mr. DeWitt pulled out a sheet of paper from the drawer and dipped his pen in the ink well.

"Now let's see...

"A set of breeches, $ 3.75   Corded Nankeen

Cotton shirting, 97 cents for two yards

A top hat, $ 3.00

Gentlemen's gloves, $1.25

Waistcoat, $ 3.90

Shoes, 90 cents

Your total cost would be $13.77."

DeWitt turned the list around for Champ to see. He picked it up and studied it.

"I had no idea it would cost so much," Champ told him, continuing to play the role of a farm hand.

With a grin, DeWitt said. "I rather though so. That's a great deal of money for a farm laborer. Is there one thing on the list you need most?"

"Will you take a gold coin?" Champ delighted in surprising the man with his question.

"Well of course. What did you decide on buying?"

"I want to buy all of it. And if you would you throw in a pair of socks and a tie?"

DeWitt decided perhaps he had misjudged this man.

He offered his hand. "My name is John DeWitt. May I ask yours?"

"My name is Champ Covington."

"Mr. Covington, forgive me, but I am not familiar with a tie?"

Champ realized again, that his research into gentlemen's dress had been very insufficient. He tried to explain that it went around a gentleman's neck under his shirt.

Mr. DeWitt's eyes brightened. "Oh, you must mean a cravat." What he laid out for Champ looked like a large napkin wrapping the neck and dropping down with a lot of frills.

"If you buy all of that, we will give you the stockings and cravat without additional cost."

Champ smiled and thanked him.

Mr. DeWitt suggested, "Try on the breeches and coat while I look for shoes that might fit you."

The new clothes were so unfamiliar. Short breeches with high stockings was the fashion. The breeches were interesting. Buttons substituted for a belt. And there was not a zipper. Probably not invented yet. The heavy coat dropped nearly to his knees. The shoes felt extremely uncomfortable. The toes were pointed and adorned with shiny brass buckles and the heels were elevated. The hat was large and reminded Champ of an admiral's hat. He felt almost like a cross-dresser.

DeWitt took the list he had made to the front counter. Champ laid his twenty-dollar gold coin beside the list. The shopkeeper he'd met at the front door, looked down at the coin as DeWitt picked it up. He commented to DeWitt that he had not seen a gold coin in quite some time. Like DeWitt, based on Champ's attire, he had made the assumption that Champ was a penniless farm laborer.

"You must have worked a very long time on the farm to have this much money." They both laughed.

"Around these parts that coin represents a fortnight's wage."

Champ did not know how to respond about the farm. "My mother left me a bit of an inheritance," Champ said with a smile.

DeWitt queried, "You may be a farmer, but you talk like a gentleman. Where do you hail from?"

"I'm from the Carolina colonies and just recently moved to these parts." Champ did not want to say too much, so took the change DeWitt handed him...six dollars and twenty-three cents.

He turned to leave as Dewitt added, "If you will take the shirting material down the block, to the tailor's, he will make you a shirt tomorrow for one dollar."

Champ thanked them and bid the storekeepers farewell. The gold coin was minted in 1782. He was glad of that. For a mere thirteen dollars and seventy-seven cents, Champ was now a gentleman!

Chapter 26

Having made his way onto the wooden boardwalk, Champ looked for Virginia. He spotted her talking with a well-dressed gentleman. She must have noticed him. She shook hands with the man and walked in his direction. When she crossed the street, she motioned for him to follow behind her. After walking for about a block she stopped and without turning around, she pointed to the boarding house, indicating that he should get a room there. She turned to walk in the opposite direction and as she passed, she whispered that she would see me at nine the next morning.

A feeling of despair hit Champ like a ton of bricks. He didn't care if she didn't want to be seen talking with him. He had to know more than that she would see him in the morning.

"Where will you be tonight?" he asked. She looked annoyed and whispered back.

"I'm going to stay at my family home. Do not worry, I'll be just fine."

To be honest, Champ wasn't worried about how *she'd* be. He was worried about how *he'd be.* Without looking at him, she continued strolling away from him up the boardwalk. The skirts of her blue print dress sashaying side to side. She looked every bit the part of a 1790's prosperous woman.

Champ looked down at his clothes again and by contrast, he looked every bit the part of a penniless farm worker, as many in this town had already assumed. The only comfort he felt came from the weight of the gold coins against his thighs.

He watched Virginia walk out of site into the crowd. For the first time since he was a small child, he felt totally insecure. As she disappeared, his life line had just been severed. What had he done? What had ever possessed him to fall into this trap? And it was a trap. He was stuck two centuries in the past. Two hundred twenty-eight years, to be exact. A chill ran through him. She had not told him *where* she would meet him. What if she did not show in the morning? If he lost contact with Virginia, he would be trapped in this time warp, and never be able to return to 2018. Bongo's words of warning came reverberating back into his brain.

At this point, he had no choice but to see if the boarding house had a room for him. Luckily, it did. His room was two dollars a night and that included an evening meal. It was supper time, so the matron pointed him to the dining room and told him to help himself.

There was only one seat available, in the middle of a table of raucous men who appeared to all be acquainted. Champ was preoccupied by fear of his situation and avoided conversation. The men made a feeble attempt to include him when he sat down, but his unresponsiveness stopped further exchange. Champ did notice that a man sitting near the end of the table periodically stared at him.

Champ decided that despite the situation, the food was very tasty. However, like the clothes, it was unfamiliar. After his stomach was sated, he headed directly up to his room, but sleep evaded him. He tossed and turned till dawn.

All he could think about was Virginia. She had directed him to dress as he had and now she was treating him like he had a contagious decease. He felt as if he had been deposited in 1791 and abandoned. If it had it in his power to return, he certainly would have done that. The other thing on his mind all night was the well-dressed man he had seen Virginia talking with. Even his brief observation of them told Champ they were known to each other.

The next morning, he put on his new clothes. The only shirt he had was the one he had traveled in, and it looked very out of place, but again, he had no choice. It was Sunday and the tailor shop would be closed. At any rate he looked better than yesterday. Perhaps it would be good enough for Virginia today.

He went down stairs to the dining room for breakfast and sat down next to the same man from the night before. He smiled at Champ and commented on his clothes.

"Very fine clothes. Are you headed to church this morning?"

It dawned on Champ that might be where Virginia and he would go when they met at nine o'clock. "I may be. I have an appointment with a certain lady. Perhaps she will take me."

Listening to the conversation at the table last night and this morning, Champ realized that his accent was detectable, so he was not surprised to notice the same man near the end of the table staring at him and listening intently to his words.

The cost of breakfast was twenty-five cents. Champ felt a little odd enjoying a hearty meal for such a low cost, so he left a ten-cent tip. Little did he know tipping was not customary in seventeen-nineties Williamsburg. It would not come into common practice in America until after the Civil War.

He had rented his room for two nights not knowing what the next day would bring with Virginia. He settled in a rocker on the porch of the boarding house and waited for her. Most people out and about in their open carriages were headed towards the church. Ladies were attired in their best dresses and beautiful bonnets. Many carried an open parasol to protect their fair skin. Some of the more affluent couples had a carriage driver.

Just as Champ was about to despair of seeing Virginia at her appointed time, he spotted her walking towards him. He stood up from the rocker and headed down the steps to greet her. When she looked up she almost did not recognize him.

"My goodness Champ, are you not the handsome one?"

"Well thank you my beautiful lady." Everything again seemed normal between them.

"You look very nice in your new clothes. Do you plan to have a new shirt made?"

"I purchased the cotton shirting and I will take it to the tailor tomorrow."

"Did you rest well last night?" she asked.

"Not really."

"Was the room not to your liking?"

"No, the room was fine. But, to be honest Virginia, lying in that boarding house room, I became aware of my dilemma, and that kept me awake the entire night.

"Dilemma?" she questioned.

"Well, if we become separated, I am marooned here, without knowledge or resources to return to my century. To be honest, it is very frightening!"

"You are thinking you would not be able to return home?"

"That is exactly what worries me. After all, you abandoned me yesterday afternoon. At least that is how it felt."

"Well, please do not concern yourself about that. I will not dessert you. We may not be together all the time, but I will always know where to find you."

"Did you stay at your old house last night?"

"No, I was surprised to learn that the house burned down last year and of course I did not know about it."

"Oh, my goodness, where did you stay?"

"I was able to stay with a neighbor," she lied.

"So, what are our plans for tonight and the rest of the time we are here?" Champ asked hoping that she would find him a place with her.

"I'm thinking you should stay where you are in the boarding house and I will try to find a room to rent nearby. It would not be proper for us to be seen together socially while living in the same building. People would gossip."

"Do you have any money?" he asked her, curious about her circumstances.

"Oh yes, I always travel with cash sewn into my dress. You needn't be concerned about that."

He was now curious about where she got money living as she did in Salem in the twenty-first century. Something to pursue with her at a later time.

"While we are all dressed up, would you like to go to church?" she asked.

"Oh, that would be nice. I noticed an Episcopal church up the street a ways," Champ offered.

"Yes. That is the Bruton Parish Church. I am familiar with it. And remember to watch your vocabulary, Champ. Try not to talk as you did in the twenty-first century."

This was going to be a bit difficult. He decided to utilize the listening powers he had honed as an author and see if he could adapt his speech.

Chapter 27

At the top of the church steps, Virginia introduced him to Minister Wyncoop.

"This is Mr. Champ Covington, visiting here from the newly formed state of South Carolina."

"We always welcome visitors, Mr. Covington. I hope you will come back next Sunday if you are still in Williamsburg. And Virginia, I am delighted to see you again. Will you be in town for a while this time?"

"Yes, I should be here for a month or so."

"Well, welcome back."

The service was rather long, but he survived and found himself observing the parishioners and the church building, which in 2018, would be on the National Historic Register.

When they left the church, he saw the man who had been talking with Virginia the day before. When the man spotted Virginia, he moved towards her, despite the fact that Champ was at her side.

"Miss Dare, I did not expect to see you again so soon. I trust you are here for a while."

Champ thought to himself that the man had spoken with Virginia only yesterday afternoon. Why was he pretending?

"My apologies Champ, this is Barrister George D'Zing a longtime friend and resident of Williamsburg. He hails from England. And George, this is my friend Mr. Champ Covington from South Carolina."

"And what is your trade Mr. Covington?"

"We have a little in common, Barrister D'Zing, I practiced law for about fifteen years before I found writing books to be a more endeavor. I sometimes miss the courtroom, but not enough to return to the law."

"What university did you attend, if I may ask?" D'Zing inquired.

"Rutgers, in New Jersey."

"You must have been there soon after the school opened. 1765 is that correct?"

"I believe that is close enough." Champ was not totally truthful. He had actually graduated from Rutgers in 1995. He wondered if Mr. D'Zing knew about Virginia's time traveling ability? Did he know about her affection for Champ? Was he one of *them*?

The Barrister continued, interrupting Champ's musings.

"I've heard the school it is one of the best. Miss Dare, I would hope that you and Mr. Covington will join me one day soon for dinner. I could have my carriage sent over for you. And may I ask, Miss Dare, where are you lodging since your family home so tragically burned?"

"I have not decided. I will have someone drop a note at your door as soon as I have an address."

They said their goodbyes. Virginia and Champ and left to find some dinner.

That afternoon, they walked around town and Virginia gave him the history she was familiar with. She found a nice room only two blocks from the boarding house. He asked her about whether she had other clothes. He suspected since her family home had burned, she might not have more than what she was wearing. She informed him that she planned to visit the tailor the next day. Champ's plan was to see Mr. DeWitt again and buy two more outfits of clothing. He surmised this would shock him and the shopkeeper even more than Champ's twenty-dollar gold piece did the day before.

That night he and Virginia went to the Williamsburg Inn for supper. It was the best eating establishment in Williamsburg at that time. They were seated at a small table with fine linen and candles. It was a very romantic setting and a first for Champ...only candles and gas lamps.

When he looked at the menu, he saw that the two of them could dine well, including a glass of wine, for less than five dollars. He admired their surroundings decided that the Williamsburg Inn catered to the elite of Williamsburg. He also noticed that gentlemen would occasionally steal glances in Virginia's direction.

After they were both served a glass of Madeira, Champ took the opportunity to ask Virginia a few questions that had been on his mind.

"Virginia, I heard you tell Mr. D'Zing that you would stay I Williamsburg for a month. You had never told me we would be here this long." Champ realized that his tone must have sounded somewhat like a whine and Virginia's formal response, confirmed his assumption.

"My apologies, Mr. Covington. I thought you might need that length of time to make your observations and collect notations for your novel." Virginia's tone told Champ that she was not fond of being questioned. However, he needed to know more than she had disclosed, so he persisted.

"Who is Mr. D'Zing?"

"I have already told you, he is an English Barrister."

"And just how do you know him?" Champ had a strong feeling that D'Zing was interested in Virginia and he had a growing sense of jealousy.

"I knew George and his wife Melander for a number of years when I was married to my third husband. We were friends until Manning and I moved to my farm in South Carolina. Soon after we left, Melander passed on and in 1793 Manning died. You saw his grave."

"I suppose he is not married?" With that question Champ feared his jealous horns were becoming obvious.

"No, Champ, I do not think so."

Champ didn't really know how Virginia felt about this man, but he could see the possibilities. If by any chance they should become involved, he could very well lose his ticket back to 2018.

"Please help me understand. You died in 1791 and your husband Manning died in 1793 and you were married at the time he died. How is that possible?"

"Oh Champ, my lives and deaths are taxing to explain. However, I will try. After I died in 1791, I mysteriously found myself able to come back to Williamsburg. I met Manning VanHouser and we were soon married. It lasted less than two years. I knew he was dying and I so took him back to South Carolina.

"Did you transport him like you did me?"

"I did. I knew his time was short and I wanted him to be with me and buried in the same cemetery as I had been buried. You saw his grave."

"Did he know you were a ghost?"

"No, he did not. Manning was too sick to even care. We landed in the little cemetery and he lived long enough for me to caress him before he took his last breath. I was able to bury him two days later in a wooden box that I built myself in the barn.

"Our time together was short, but happy. He was such a sweet man."

"What about your two other husbands. Did either of them know about your...your abilities?" Champ persisted with his interrogation.

"Yes, Champ," she said with a little less patience. "I did tell both of them. And like you, they were skeptical. And like you, they went along with me. In the end, I was always sorry I told them."

"And why is that?" Champ queried.

"Once they knew about, shall I say, my skills, they never trusted me completely. If I was out of their sight for only a short time, they thought I had traveled...if you know what I mean. And before you ask, yes both of them died a natural death while living on the farm."

"Your husband, James Thornhill was in the civil war, right?"

"Correct. It was very sad. James was a broken man when he came home from the fighting. Some of the men he fought with brought him all the way home in a hay wagon. He had been shot twice and nearly lost his right arm. He recovered but was never able to do what he called a day's work. Six years later he died. I'm convinced he never recovered from depression after the war." She went on to tell Champ about her other husband. He assumed she sensed that would be his next question.

"William McGregor was a fine man and a wonderful farmer. He was a true patriot. He organized the men around our area into a platoon. Then they joined the American Revolution. Because he had initiated the platoon, they made him captain. When he returned home four years later, he was very proud of this new country they had fought to create.

"William loved to hunt on weekends. When he was not tilling the earth, he was hunting. One fall, he and a friend went bear hunting in the mountains behind our farm. I was told by his friend, that they treed a large black bear. According to his friend, the bear had climbed out onto a dry limb and while William was standing under the tree preparing to shoot, the limb snapped under the weight of the bear and he hit the ground right in front of William. William got off one shot, but it was not fatal. The bear came after him and slapped him in the head before William's hunting partner could get off a killing shot. He died hours later from a broken neck. He was such a fine man. It took me a long time to move past my grief."

"Help me understand. You were born in 1751 and William was born in 1768, nineteen years later. So, he was significantly younger than you?"

"Champ, I'm able to go forward in years as well as go back."

This information stunned Champ. Every time this woman opened her mouth, out came more incredible tales. No wonder her two husbands did not trust her after her revelations. Like him, they probably never fully comprehended. Virginia continued talking about William.

"In this case I went forward in years and that was when I met him. However, he did out live me by 38 years. We never had children. That saddens me, but perhaps, given these unusual abilities of mine, it is best not to pass them on to yet another generation. I'm not sure I'm even interested in another marriage."

For several minutes, Champ just sat there stunned. Finally, he had to confirm what she had just told him.

"So, bottom line is, you can use your powers to go forward or backward in time."

"That is true. What I cannot do is travel into the future beyond the present day in 2018."

Champ had had enough surprises from Virginia that day and was ready to escape back to his boarding house room. The restaurant was closing as they left, and they agreed to meet for dinner after they both did the necessary trips to the tailor and mercantile. He was still trying to remember that 'dinner' was what he had always called 'lunch'; and 'supper' was what he had always known as 'dinner', the evening meal. As difficult as it was going back, Champ chuckled at the thought of how difficult it would be for one of these colonial Williamsburg residents to travel *forward* in time. How would they comprehend cars, television or 'flying machines', much less space travel? Perhaps going back in time was not as bad as it had seemed to him in the past twenty-four hours.

****

Champ pulled three twenty-dollar coins from the seams of his pants. That would more than cover the cost of two more sets of clothing, plus money for boarding and food for the week. He knew better than to carry all his coins around in his breeches. The most logical thing to do was to find a bank and deposit the rest. After Virginia's recent revelations and peculiar behavior, that money was becoming increasingly important to him.

Monday morning, he went to the dry goods store and was greeted enthusiastically by Mr. DeWitt. He and the proprietor were impressed that Champ was back to purchase two more complete outfits. This time he was going to see if there were more comfortable shoes among their collection. After careful selection of his purchases, the two shopkeepers were almost giddy when he produced two more twenty-dollar gold coins.

This was the beginning of his third day in colonial Williamsburg and he had spent a total of forty-eight dollars on food, logging and three new sets of clothes. He now had only nineteen hundred and fifty-two dollars remaining in his pants. It dawned on him that since he could not be certain of how long Virginia intended to keep him there, it would be critical that he conserve his money.

Before Champ completed his purchases, he casually asked Mr. DeWitt about the town of Williamsburg and its establishments. It was his circuitous way of finding out about what banking institution might reside in the town.

DeWitt was a very prideful citizen of his hometown. He went on and on. Although Champ had not intended to hear about Williamsburg in such embellished detail, he did find it fascinating. It was exactly what Virginia had proposed. He would learn first-hand about the history of his country. This thought had distracted him slightly from Mr. DeWitt's monologue, but he was brought back instantly when he heard the shopkeeper mention The First Bank of the United States, which had been chartered within that very month in 1791. He listened politely for a few more minutes and then thanked Mr. DeWitt, making the excuse that he had an appointment with a beautiful woman. They both smiled knowingly and invited him back, 'anytime'.

Champ made straight away for the new national banking institution. It was not the stately bank building he might have envisioned for this historic town. There were no marble floors or columns. It looked like a hastily converted store front. After all, the Congress in Philadelphia had only chartered The First Bank of the United States very recently. There was however, a guard inside the front door. He looked me up and down as Champ entered. He was glad he had on my new clothes, but still embarrassed for the old shirt. The tailor would be his next stop. If he had come in wearing my old farmer clothes, he most likely would have been tossed out onto the muddy street.

Despite the temporary look of the bank building, Champ did notice that the tellers were dressed very formally in black business suits of the day. Some things never change!

"How may I help you sir?" a middle-aged teller inquired in a very formal tone.

"I would like to open an account with the bank."

"And do you live in Williamsburg, sir?"

"I recently relocated to Williamsburg and am temporarily residing at the Johnson Boarding House on Lafayette."

"May I have your name and a reputable reference, please?"

The second request was one Champ had not anticipated.

My legal name is Howard Covington, Jr., but my friends all call me Champ. My reference is Barrister George D'Zing.

"Quite a fine reference for someone new to town, Mr. Covington. And just how do you know Barrister D'Zing?"

"He is in the law profession and I am a lawyer as well."

"Very well Mr. Covington." Evidently, he had satisfied either the teller's curiosity or the bank's security questions, and Champ was now approved.

"How much would you like to deposit today?"

"I wish to deposit eighteen hundred dollars," Champ responded.

"And what form of tender will you be depositing with us today, Mr. Covington?"

At first, he did not understand his question, then he realized the teller wanted to know if he had the new paper money just recently issued by the Congress in Philadelphia or another type of tender.

"I have gold coin in the amount of nineteen-hundred and fifty-two dollars. As I indicated, I would like to deposit eighteen hundred dollars. I would like to receive the difference of one hundred and fifty-two dollars in paper currency."

Champ detected a quizzical smile on the teller's face that did not extend to his eyes.

"That is a rather large sum of gold coins. We do not see much of that around here," he said cautiously.

Before leaving the boarding house this morning, Champ had carefully removed all the coins from where he had sewn them into his pants and placed them in a small bag, he had purchased at the mercantile the first day. He laid the bag on the counter. The teller emptied the bag and stacked the coins up in groups. He counted them three times before he was satisfied of the correct amount. Champ was given a record of his deposit and an envelope with four blank checks which he could use to make purchases if I desired. Finally, the teller handed him one hundred and fifty-two dollars back in paper money and thanked him for his business.

During this transaction, the large amount of gold coins on the teller's counter had attracted the attention of the bank manager. He stood behind the teller and observed. When the transaction was complete, and Champ had placed the dollar bills in the inside pocket of his waistcoat, the manager came from around the teller cages and introduced himself.

"Mr. Covington, my name is Edward Hallock. I am the bank manager. I wanted to thank you for displaying faith in the First Bank of the United States. You may feel confident that your money is safely deposited and will be available to you at any time."

"I am confident my money is quite secure, Mr. Hallock. Thank you."

"Once you are settled, please drop by. I would be honored to dine with you."

Chapter 28

Champ arrived just before twelve o'clock at Christina Campbell's Tavern on Waller Street near the intersection of Lafayette Street. He asked for a table at the window. Both Waller Street and Lafayette were a tangle of horse-drawn wagons, fancy carriages, men on horseback, and ladies walking among all the hub-bub. It gave traffic jams a whole new image for Champ. He almost felt like he was watching a movie set from the director's chair.

At first, he did not recognize the beautiful woman as Virginia, as he saw her approaching through the crowded street. What a lovely sight she was, wearing a beautiful dress tightly fitted around her waist. Her breasts were pushed up and partially exposed, which surprisingly was the fashion of the day. A matching cloak was draped over her shoulders and hung loosely at her sides.

Her dress was made of a lustrous silk material. The pattern was a blend of twirling burgundies and gold. Champ stood as she approached the table.

"Virginia, you look absolutely stunning. How were you able to have such a beautiful dress tailored in such a short time?"

"Thank you for your agreeable compliment. I actually found the dress in a shop on Lafayette Street. The tailor had made it to display in his window. After explaining my predicament, he agreed to sell it to me. He fitted it very quickly."

Purchasing his clothes and opening a bank account along having his shirt made, were Champ's only tasks that day; and as he sat in the tavern, waiting for Virginia, he found himself feeling at loose ends. He had nothing to occupy his time and knew none of Virginia's plans that might include him. He needed to pin her down a little more. He thought a good idea would be to invite her for supper that night.

"Thank you Champ, but I believe I'll stay in tonight. The lady of the house invited me to sup with her."

Normally this was no big deal. However, Champ was here as *her* guest. At least in the beginning that had been his impression. He still felt insecure and did not want to be away from her very long at a time. It dawned on him that he was beginning to feel like the men she had described when she was telling about her three husbands. She must have been reading his mind again.

"I have a suggestion for you Champ. Williamsburg is a good-sized town and seeing it on foot takes a lot of walking. Tomorrow, why don't you go to one of the livery stables, rent a horse and explore the area. I think you might enjoy that."

"What about you? Will you join me?" I asked hopefully.

"Not this time, Champ. I really need to get some riding clothes. Perhaps in a week or so."

A week or so! Was he not going to see her for a whole week? What could she possibly be doing with her time? Spending it with that barrister guy? Champ decided not to say anything more for fear of alienating her totally.

When they finished dinner, they sat outside on a bench. For winter, it was a mild and sunny day. Virginia was quiet, and her behavior seemed a little distant. It could have been his imagination, but he didn't think so. After all, since he had met her, there was only one time when she demonstrated any affection. That had been when she told him she loved him. She had never uttered that sentiment again.

"Virginia, can you give me an idea when you think we will return home?" The expression on her face was blank and she did not immediately respond.

"Perhaps in a fortnight. Are you growing homesick already?"

"Not necessarily, but you have not shared any plans since we arrived. I am the type of person who plans ahead and as you know I am very vulnerable here."

"Keep one thing in mind, Champ. When we return we will arrive only minutes from the time we left. It will be the same day and time we left. So, you will not miss anything."

Champ thought, "She either doesn't get it, or she is deflecting my concern about being abandoned." Either way her aloof behavior was beginning to irritate him.

Without another word, she stood and headed toward her rooming house.

She had indicated she might not see him for a week. What would he do with his time? Well, being of a pragmatic nature, he decided to experience 18th century as she had originally suggested...unfortunately on his own.

****

Champ had not even caught sight of her in town for two days, so out of boredom on Wednesday, he found a livery stable and rented a horse. He told the man that he had not ridden in a long time, so maybe he could arrange for a gentle horse. It took some getting used to, so Champ kept to the back streets where he only encountered foot-travelers.

After riding up and down streets throughout the town for several hours, he found he was actually enjoying this historic settlement. He spotted a sandy road that led away from the center of Williamsburg and decided to explore further. Large oaks lined the road on either side and the bare branches of winter created a canopy through which the sunlight filtered. He passed a number of gentlemen heading towards town and they tipped their hats. About a mile down the road, a white fence bordered the road on the right. The fence continued down the road as far as Champ could see, and a number of thoroughbred horses nibbled the green grass that had emerged along the fence posts. It was a beautiful piece of property, and from the expanse of the fence, it must comprise hundreds of acres.

Eventually, he noticed in the distance what looked like an entrance to a grand estate. As Champ approached the drive up to the house, he spotted an elaborate sign that read, 'D'Zing Estate'. "Wow", Champ thought, "George must have a very successful law practice. Out of my league for sure."

Champ wondered if he had trespassed on his private property along that sandy road and decided it was prudent to reverse his path. He had ridden far enough for one day, so headed back to the livery stable. It was nearly five o'clock and this time of year in late winter, it would be dark soon. The young attendant at the stable was leaning against a wall, Champ figured the boy was waiting for him to return so he could go home. He apologized and paid him a little extra for his trouble. He did not call it a tip. He had learned his lesson about tipping at the boarding house.

Supper was served at the boarding house from five o'clock to six o'clock, so by the time he walked from the livery, supper would be over. He had not had a drink in over a week, so when he passed the King's Tavern on North Henry he decided to experience yet one more establishment that day. The tavern was crowded. Champ made his way through the throng and noticed a man vacating his seat at the end of the bar. Ale appeared to be the drink of the time, so he asked for Ale.

"What size you want sir?" The barkeep asked.

Champ was not sure what the term was for ordering a mug of ale back in 1791 so he replied, "Give me one just like the fellow sitting next to me."

"Very well sir, one pint of ale."

It only took one sip for him to remember that the English drank warm beer. This was indeed warm and would take some practice to appreciate. The gas lights created a dim glow and it took his eyes a while to adjust. Taverns had not changed much in over two hundred years. The place was noisy, and the air was rank with smoke from cigars and pipes.

When the barkeep brought his pint, the gentleman to his right turned and raised his pint with a welcoming smile

"Ah, my good man. Did I detect a bit of an accent?

Champ smiled back and teased, "Just what kind of accent do you detect? I did not realize I had one."

"I do not believe it is a Boston or Philadelphia accent. Perhaps south of here?" he guessed. "Never seen you in here before so I know you must have just arrived in Williamsburg. If I might be so bold, from where do you hail?"

"The last place I lived was in the newly formed state of South Carolina."

"You don't say! How long you been in Williamsburg?"

"A little less than a week," Champ confessed.

"And what is your trade?"

"I practice law."

Champ knew he meant well, but so many questions!

"Sir, you might be surprised to learn that you are not the only one from that state of South Carolina." That startled me.

"James Vance, sitting down near the other end of the bar. I believe he told me he hailed from South Carolina. I only talked to the man once. He doesn't seem to be a sociable sort, you know, and has a little too much to drink most nights. He lives in a cheap room behind this building somewhere. Go introduce yourself to him but know you have been warned about his moody nature."

Champ looked in the direction of the man his acquaintance had pointed out. He was about Champ's age and might have been rather handsome, except he wore such a very tired face. He decided he would bide his time and perhaps introduce himself another day.

****

It was now Thursday and the third day in a row that Champ had not seen Virginia. The gamut of emotions running through him stretched from loneliness, to anger, to frustration. What was he to do if he never saw her again?

He wasted his day walking aimlessly around the main streets and late in the afternoon he planted himself on the bench under the statue on Lafayette Street, where he had joined Virginia that first day. From that vantage point, he could see the greatest majority people. In desperation, he decided to go to the rooming house where she had taken a room. When the lady of the house opened the door, Champ was told that Miss Dare had decided, after two nights, to move elsewhere. Why had she not told him she was moving? Something was wrong...very, very wrong.

Chapter 29

Thursday night was a sleepless one for Champ. He was consumed with worry and frustration, taking out his angst on his pillow. Had Virginia abandoned him on purpose? He did not know where to turn for help. If he told anybody how he had arrived in Williamsburg, he would be laughed out of town. He did have money in the bank, but that would not last forever. Did he need to think about finding employment? His knowledge of the colonial era law, was minimal at best. The only lawyer he knew was the Barrister, and he certainly would not approach the barrister about employment. "I *will not!*" he said out loud to no one.

He spent most of the morning catnapping, in an attempt to make up for the night before. By late afternoon he was getting cabin fever, so he left the boarding house and headed for Kings Tavern. Champ decided he needed a drink, and more importantly, someone to talk to. Perhaps it was time to introduce himself to James Vance, from South Carolina. At this point, he didn't care if the man was grumpy or inebriated. Anybody would do! When he walked in, the big crowd had not arrived, so Champ had his choice of seats at the bar.

He was about to select his seat when a fellow at the other end of the bar called out and nodded toward the bar stool next to him. Said he had something to ask Champ.

On second glance, Champ remembered him from the previous night. He took a seat and extended his hand.

"Champ Covington," he offered.

"James Vance," he told me. "I noticed you last night. You stood out to me because of your hair. Nobody around here wears hair that short."

He paused and looked Champ up and down. He figured he had encountered Vance early enough that he had not yet imbibed heavily. However, Champ could still smell an awful odor about his body. After a few moments of silence between the two men, as they sipped their beers, Champ spoke. "I understand that you claim to be from South Carolina."

"Correct. I was told you are as well. Is that right?" Vance replied cautiously.

"I am indeed," Champ confirmed.

In addition to the aroma that surrounded Vance, Champ also noticed that Vance was not dressed as well as others, and assumed he was more laborer than gentry.

Champ was pleased that Vance had approached him and decided that even though they were separated by two centuries, at least, however remote, they might have a little in common.

"Whatever brings you up here? It's long ways to travel by horse or wagon." Vance commented.

Champ almost laughed out loud. If Vance only knew how he had arrived.

"I practice law and write books. A lady friend suggested I come and experience Williamsburg first hand." This was mostly the truth, just not the entire truth.

"If you write books," Vance commented. "I could give you a story, but nobody would ever believe it."

"I write mostly fiction so that could be good material," Champ joked.

Vance smiled at this remark.

"Let's save it for another time," Vance said with bitterness in his voice.

Over several pints of ale, Champ shared his discoveries of Williamsburg and asked Vance questions about the area. Finally, they began to explore commonalities. Vance asked him where in South Carolina he came from.

"In the Blue Ridge Mountains," Champ told him. "How about you?"

"I lived near there, in a little community of Salem."

"Are you kidding me? I live just outside of Salem. O.K. I told you why I'm up here, now it's your turn," Champ queried.

"I was dating a woman and she talked me into coming up here and I have never been back," he said sourly.

"You know how women can be. You must have been in love with her at the time and I am guessing that you did not marry her?"

"No! I never got the chance. Soon after we got here, she disappeared."

Warning bells went off in Champ's head. This was too much of a coincidence. Champ lapsed into silence and just stared at himself in the mirror behind the bar. What he saw staring back, was a fool!

What a twist of fate. Vance was from Salem, and he had come up here with a woman who had walked out on him, the same way Virginia appeared to be abandoning Champ.

While Vance's appearance and body odor would lead one to believe he was a common laborer, he talked like an educated man. Champ decided to probe, to either quell his suspicions or to confirm them.

"Vance, how long have you lived here?" Champ finally asked.

"Oh, I guess around six or seven years."

Champ changed the subject not sure he wanted the answers he thought he might get. So, they made small talk or merely sat in silence for some time. But after both had consumed numerous pints, Champ threw caution to the wind.

"Was Salem just a crossroad when you left it?" Champ asked.

"Not exactly, there was a school and several churches, a grocery store and an Ace Hardware." The look on his face told Champ he felt he had made a mistake in sharing that last bit.

"An Ace Hardware? Do you remember the year you left to come up here?" Champ queried.

Vance's face darkened. He did not answer. Here merely lowered his head and stared into his ale. Champ could tell something was wrong. Then under his breath he whispered that he did not remember the year.

Champ changed the subject and asked him what kind of work he did.

"I'm a little ashamed, but soon after I got here, I ran out of money. I had to find whatever kind of work I could get to support myself. So, I work about a mile from here for a tanner. It is nasty and smelly work. But it was all I could find."

That explained why he had that unpleasant odor about him, thought Champ.

****

It was now Saturday. Almost a week had passed since Virginia had walked down North Henry Street and out of Champ's sight. He felt like he was coming to the end of his rope. If he had been dropped off on Mars, it would not have felt much different, he thought. He had vanished from his cabin on Gap Hill Road and was now living 228 years in the past.

Sunday morning, Champ attended church. His hope was that Virginia would be there. She was not! Neither was George D'Zing. He shook the minister's hand and the minister remembered him. Champ did not ask, and the minister did not mention Virginia's name. Could she have gone back to Salem and left him?

Late Monday afternoon Champ again headed for King's Tavern. This was becoming a place in Williamsburg where he felt comfortable. The people in there reminded him of the patrons at Bob's Place. He hoped James Vance would be there because he suspected his story and

Champ's, were inexorably connected. He needed to ask him a few more questions. Vance was not there when he arrived, so he sat at the end of the bar where there were several empty stools. Champ had not been there long when Vance walked through the door. He looked pleased to see Champ, sat down on the adjacent stool and ordered a pint. They made small talk for a few minutes. Champ could tell Vance was about to ask a question. Evidently, they both had questions.

"Champ, since we talked last week, I have needed to ask you one question."

Warning bells went off in Champ's head. He knew the question Vance was going to ask, and he *did not* want him to ask it. All Champ could manage was "Go ahead."

"What was the name of the woman that came with you to Williamsburg?"

Champ could not answer him. He did not want the name to be what he knew in his gut it would be. Vance was reading the emotion on Champ's face, so he offered, "Let me throw out a name. Was it Virginia Dare?"

There must have been a look of astonishment on Champ's face. And Vance knew immediately that it was Virginia who had transported him.

"Oh my God! Champ, she has brought three of us here from the Salem area. Champ you are the third."

The voices of Big Bongo and Little Tom Tatum were shouting their warnings in his head. The connection between Vance and Champ were confirmed. Also confirmed was the fact that Champ was definitely marooned 228 years before his time.

"James, do you know the other man she brought here?" Champ asked.

"I do know him, but rarely do I ever see him."

"Does he still live around here?"

"As far as I know he does," Vance replied.

"How did you meet or discover the way both of you arrived in Williamsburg?"

"I met him here in the Kings Tavern. He had no money and I observed him get thrown out because he couldn't pay for his ale. I paid for the pint and followed him outside. I picked up on the haircut just as I did with you. What scares me is that there may be more of us transported back here."

The more they talked the more despondent Champ became. He had additional questions.

"What was the name of the third man? Champ asked.

"Francis Morrow," Vance told him.

"What happened to him?"

"When Francis arrived, he had only cash that was being used the day he left Salem. It was worthless here. When he tried to use it, he was suspected of trying to pass off illegitimate money. He nearly found himself penniless. He was wearing a very expensive Rolex watch which he was able to sell for the gold it contained.

"But people soon became suspicious of the origin of such a watch. That's why he could not get credit or a job. After staying for a couple of nights at the boarding house, he was broke, and hungry. When he was accused of stealing vegetables to sustain himself, he was arrested and thrown into jail. He was in there for a month before a judge sentenced him to one week in the stocks at the city square to be publicly shamed. Then he was branded on his forehead with the letter 'T' for theft. I had been thrown into my own difficulties and had no financial resources to help him.

"Eventually someone took pity on him, or took advantage of him, one of the two. They gave him a job working on a farm for only food and lodging. He makes no money beyond that. The last time I saw him, he had let his hair grow down over his forehead to hide the brand."

"James, I think we should try to locate Morrow and talk about our mutual situation."

"We can do that, but I don't think it will change our situation," Vance said.

"I think I know your answer, but James, have you seen Virginia recently?" His answer surprised me.

"I do see her on rare occasion. A number of years ago after I first got here, I would try to talk to her, but now I steer clear of her with good reason. Actually, I saw her about three or four days ago."

"When and where did you see her?" Champ asked excitedly.

"I believe it was last Monday. I saw her going into a dress shop."

"I was with her that day and we had lunch together," Champ told Vance. "That was the last time I saw her. You said you don't try to approach her anymore. Why?"

"I had a major run in with her boyfriend George."

"Do you mean Georgia D'Zing?" Champ didn't want Vance to confirm that question either. This reference to D'Zing as her *boyfriend*, had been on Champ's mind for some time. Vance's answer confirmed his suspicions and told him that he was doomed, just as Vance and Morrow had been, to live out the rest of their natural lives in colonial Williamsburg.

"Yes, the Barrister. I warn you Champ. Don't go near that son-of-a-bitch. He is the reason I have never been able to get a decent job."

"Tell me about that," Champ asked with interest.

"Soon after I arrived here, I lost track of her within a few days, just like you have. We had almost been like lovers, but we never made love at her farm. I felt she was offering me a wonderful adventure to go back to the past and I felt my prospects looked good to have a roll in the hay. I should have let my brain do my thinking, and not my dick.

"Francis Morrow and I speculated that she could not travel through time without bringing someone with her. That would explain why she took three husbands back to her farm in Salem. I'm sure you saw their graves. They were her ticket back to the farm and we, of course, were her ticket back here to Williamsburg. I don't know who she took back to the farm the last three times, but I suspect that if you found three zombies in or around Salem, they would be the ones." A sad smile briefly crossed Vance's face.

"You said D'Zing kept you from getting a job. What happened?" Champ asked.

"Soon after she abandoned me, I became frantic. I was like a wild man. Like I said, when I did see Virginia, she would blow me off or disappear. One day a couple of weeks after I arrived, I saw her and D'Zing in an open carriage. I had this feeling that he was the reason for her leaving me stranded and I was really angry. I ran out into the street and jumped up on the step of the carriage as it was moving.

"I screamed at Virginia. That son-of-a-bitch George took his horse whip and struck me in the face, ordering me to get off his carriage. The whip cut my face and I was bleeding. The carriage stopped, and he told me that I was going to be arrested. That night the Deputy Sheriff came to the boarding house and hauled me off to jail. I was stuck behind bars for five days. Finally, the sheriff released me without any charges. I'm telling you Champ, D'Zing has a lot of influence in this town. Do not cross him!

Chapter 30

Now Champ knew where Virginia had gone. The question was, would she see him? After Vance's revelation, he was not certain. And there was a strong possibility of having a confrontation with the bastard George D'Zing. That would only serve to get him into troubles similar to those of Vance and Morrow.

Vance's advice had been to steer clear of D'Zing. However, Champ could not resist trying to reason with Virginia. So, he rented the horse again and headed out the road leading to the D'Zing Estate. It was mid-afternoon on Saturday when he tied his horse up in front of the big house. It was a typical Georgian Williamsburg mansion with four tall marble columns. Only an extremely wealthy man could afford an estate like this. It was no wonder that Virginia would be attracted to George. He was a tall, handsome man who wore a grey wig tied back in a pigtail and secured with a ribbon.

A butler, dressed in a white coat, answered the door when Champ knocked.

"Yes sir, may I tell the master who is calling?"

"Please tell him that Lawyer Covington is calling."

The door was left slightly ajar. The butler returned and told him the master would see him in the library. Upon entering, he could see how well appointed the home was, with exquisite furniture, probably brought over from Europe.

The butler opened two ten-foot, ornately carved oak doors, exposing a lavish library with hundreds of leather-bound volumes. As Champ entered, George rose from his chair.

"Well, well Mr. Covington, what a pleasure it is to see you again. I believe it was two or three Sundays ago that we met at church."

They shook hands and he offered Champ a chair near the open fire.

"Yes, it was at the church where Virginia and I attended. It was a very nice service. I believe it was the first time I have ever attended an Episcopal church."

"Well I do hope you will consider returning."

It appeared D'Zing was not anxious to extend pleasantries with me, and he cut to the chase.

"Mr. Covington, I surmise you are here on business? Are you looking for a good lawyer?" He laughed at his own joke.

"Yes, Barrister D'Zing, I am here on business. Business of grave importance to me."

"Please proceed." Just as Virginia had kept a blank face when Champ had asked her about returning to Salem, D'Zing kept the same expressionless face.

"As you probably know, Virginia brought me here on what I now consider false pretenses."

"False pretenses?" he mimicked.

"Yes, she painted a beautiful picture of the two of us coming back here together so that I might develop material for a new book. My claim of false pretenses is because only days after arriving, she disappeared. My guess is that since you know her well, you must also know that others have been deceived by similar temptations and have been stranded in a place where we are having a difficult time surviving. We simply want to return back to where we came from. That is all we want."

"I hear what you are saying, but how do you perceive I can help you."

"I would like your assistance in persuading Virginia to return all three gentlemen to South Carolina. I assume there are only three of us."

"I am unsure that I am capable of that task, Mr. Covington."

"If you are unwilling Mr. D'Zing, I would like to try. Please let me speak with her."

"She is not here, and I do not think she would speak to you."

"Why do you say that? I have caused her no harm. I only want to know how to go back home. Surely you understand my request."

"Mr. Covington, I have absolutely no control over her. What she does, she does on her own.

"Mr. D'Zing, I implore you to ask her to talk with me. No harm will come to anyone. I merely need to appeal to her sense of decency." Champ stopped for a moment, not quite sure what else he could say to convince D'Zing to help him. Then he thought of a tactic.

"Barrister, I am aware that the two of you, uh...care about each very much. I am not trying to come between you. Quite to the contrary I hope the two of you are very happy. I would presume that it would benefit you personally, if the three men Virginia brought to Williamsburg with her, were no longer an obstacle?"

D'ZIng's voice gained a few octaves and his face blushed. "You talk as if you think she is here. She is not here. Precisely why do you think she is in this house?"

"I have first-hand experience with her ability appear and disappear in a room. The second reason I believe she is here is that an acquaintance informed me they had seen the two of you traveling in your carriage in the direction of this estate. I am confident that she is in this house, if not in this room, at this very minute." Champ let that accusation hang in the air.

It was then that D'Zing lost his cool. His voice boomed, as does a lawyer's when making an argument in the court room.

"Covington, you will not stand here in my home and impugn my veracity. I do not wish to ever see you again and if that happens, there will be charges brought against you for slander. I forbid you to ever return. I also forbid you to make any attempt to speak with my future wife."

"Now, hold on Barrister. If you recall, I was admitted into your home with your approval. I did not force my way in. I have made no threats. You are not the only barrister in this library, Mr. D'Zing. And I just may have a better understanding of American law than the foreigner you are. Do not forget the prestigious university from which I graduated...at the top of my class.

"Heaven forbid there is a time when Miss Dare persuades you to travel with her to her home in South

Carolina. I can assure you that you will be received with far more respect than I have been afforded here today."

Champ was proud that he still maintained his skill in courtroom banter, but he unfortunately, because he had been insulted and threatened, he had allowed himself to display his anger. He knew he had made a few good points, and it appeared they made an impact with D'Zing. He looked rather startled. And now was the time for Champ's final trick.

"Virginia, I know you are in this room and I am confident you have heard every word. I want you to know, this is not a threat, but a promise. If I ever find my way back home, I will personally dig up your grave and scatter your bones to the wind. Your tombstone will be crushed and used in the foundation of a new out-house for your mother. You will forever lose your ability to time travel and perpetrate evil as you have done for several hundred years. It is time this comes to an end, Miss Virginia!

D'Zing screamed at the top of his lungs,

"Get out!! Get out of my house you bastard! Get out!!" He pointed his long finger at the butler, "Johnson, show this man to the door and never, ever receive him again."

As the door was opened for Champ, he said politely, "Thank you, Johnson."

Champ's rebuttal to D'Zing had created an explosion of pompous anger in the man. But Champ was as pissed as he had ever been. If Virginia had planned to help him return, that door had now been closed.

Champ mounted his horse, but before he got out of earshot, he heard the piercing voice of Virginia.

In a rage, she shouted, "George, what have you done?"

Champ pointed his horse towards Williamsburg and rode without a single glance back.

Chapter 31

On Saturday afternoon, a couple of days after his altercation with D'Zing, Champ was sitting in the boarding room's parlor making notes on a piece of paper he had been given by the proprietor. These long-hand notes with pen and ink were not an easy task for someone who was accustomed to Ctrl Z and spell check on a laptop. Computers were now in his past, and ironically in the future for everyone else. "Isn't that paradoxical," thought Champ.

From here he could see the William & Mary School of Law. He had heard the campus covered twelve hundred acres. Several young men, whom he assumed were students of the University, stood with an older gentleman on the boardwalk just outside where Champ sat in the parlor. He overheard the older gentleman remark to the students, "That tall red-headed fellow is Mr. Thomas Jefferson. He helped build the framework of our new nation."

Thomas Jefferson! Champ jumped up out of his chair to see if he could spot him. Champ momentarily forgot his predicament in his eagerness to see one of his personal heroes, in flesh and blood.

He crossed the street and positioned himself within earshot of the boys clustered around Jefferson. Champ had read that Jefferson attended William & Mary in 1760 and graduated at the age of sixteen at the top of his class. As they moved along the boardwalk, he could tell that they were discussing horticulture. Jefferson was explaining how to crossbreed certain strains of fruit trees to create superior fruit. Jefferson was 43 years old when Champ listened in on that impromptu lecture. What a life this brilliant young man had before him. Only a decade from then, he would become President of the United States, Champ thought.

This experience reminded Champ of a quote from a speech by President Kennedy at the White House. He was talking to a group of Nobel Prize winners:

> *"I think this is the most extraordinary collection of talent...that has ever been gathered together at the White House, with the possible exception of when Thomas Jefferson dined alone."*

What an amazing opportunity to see this great man, Champ thought. This was only the second experience he had truly enjoyed in Williamsburg.

****

After seeing Mr. Jefferson, Champ headed over to the Kings Tavern. He was quite certain that James Vance would admonish him for confronting D'Zing at his home.

As was usually the case on Saturday afternoon, the tavern was full of raucous men and a loud balladeer singing his heart out for coins thrown at his feet. Champ looked around the smoky room for Vance. He spotted him sitting at a small table in the corner by himself.

"Hey Champ. It's good to see you. Find another chair and join me."

Champ asked a barmaid to locate one, and he joined Vance. He avoided talking about what he had done for as long as he could. Instead, he initiated the conversation by asking about Francis Morrow.

"Have you found out where he is?" Champ asked.

"Actually, I have." Vance admitted. "He is working on a farm about ten miles north of town."

Champ was excited at that news. "You know tomorrow is Sunday. I would guess he will not be working, so let's ride out there and pay him a visit. What do you say?"

"I'm sorry Champ, but I don't own a horse. Otherwise I would very much like to go out and see Francis."

"I don't own one either. I'll rent two horses at the livery," Champ offered.

"Champ, I don't want to put you in financial difficulties by spending money frivolously."

"Vance, do not worry about the money. We really need to find a way to get back to our own time. Perhaps by getting our three heads together, we can find a way out of here."

Champ needed to tell Vance about his visit with D'Zing, and decided he'd waited long enough. So, he dove in and relayed the whole story. He found that in the retelling, he was still angry.

Vance responded as Champ had expected he would.

"All I can tell you, Champ is to watch your back. D'Zing is vindictive, and when you are not alert, he will try to even the score. The threat you made about Virginia will stick in his head. He may try anything to get the upper hand with you. I'm afraid I am not as optimistic as you about returning to Salem. I can't imagine how we would we do it without Virginia."

"I don't know right now how we get back, but we have to do something."

****

Sunday morning, he met Vance at the livery and he rented horses for the both of them. The ride north was a pleasant one. They passed wagons and buggies with families headed to church and slaves on foot headed to worship with their families.

After two hours, they came to a sign that read: Wood-Lewis Farm. It was a beautiful setting, with the winter wheat at its prime. They followed a bend in the road and came upon a two-story farmhouse. They saw no one around the grounds. Champ assumed that was because this was Sunday. Not far from the main house Vance pointed out several small shacks. They headed toward these buildings, assuming they were housing for the farmhands and slaves. Under a massive oak tree sat an old man, carving a staff.

Vance called out a greeting. The old man looked up and nodded. We drew up our horses and asked the man if Francis Morrow could be found on this farm?

"Ya, he down 'der a cuttin' fire wood fer his stove."

Champ spotted a man about a hundred yards from them, cutting limbs off a dead log.

He noticed them as they approached and halted his work.

Vance called out, "Hey Francis, you workin' on Sunday?"

A broad smile broke across the man's face. The first thing Champ noticed was hair hanging down over the man's forehead like the teenagers of the 21st century. It was then he remembered the branded 'T'.

"Well I'll be! Is that you Vance?" called out Morrow.

"It is at that, Francis. Since you don't ever come to town, I had to come see you. I want you to meet my friend Champ Covington. He is a new comer to town."

"Nice to meet you Mr. Covington. And Vance, you should remember that I don't come to town, because I don't have a horse and no coin for my pint of ale. I'm pretty much stuck here." His bitterness matched what Champ had heard from Vance when relaying his situation.

"If you got time, Champ and I would like to visit with you. The three of us got a lot in common, if you know what I mean."

With that, Francis looked up sharply and gave Champ the once-over.

"I got all day. It's Sunday and other than cutting myself a little fire wood, I'm all yours."

Vance and Champ dismounted, and the three men settled themselves in the sunshine under a nearby tree. Vance got right to the point.

"It turns out that Champ arrived in Williamsburg a few weeks back the same way you and I did."

"You don't say?" Francis said, shaking his head and putting a sympathetic hand on Champ's arm. "I'm sorry man," he said.

Vance continued, "I told him about you and he wanted to come out this morning and meet you. Francis, I don't have a horse either, but Champ was very insistent about meeting you. He actually rented us both horses for this trip. It turns out the Dare woman brought all three of us here from Salem."

Champ asked Francis how long he had been in Williamsburg.

"Champ, I have lost track of time, but maybe around ten years. I expect I will die here and be buried out at the end of that big field in an unmarked grave like other farmworkers."

It was plain to see Morrow felt his situation was hopeless. His pay was less than a dollar a day, and half of that was held back for his food and lodging.

Champ had an idea that he had been mulling over while they rode. He had not yet discussed his thoughts with Vance. This was the perfect time to share it with his two companions. However, as Champ opened his mouth to begin, something made him change my mind. He decided it might be prudent to wait for another time.

"Francis would you consider coming into town next Sunday?" Champ asked. "If you would, I will give you four dollars to be used to catch a ride into town. We can drink our pints and talk about a plan I'm formulating. We could meet at the Kings Tavern around two o'clock and I will arrange to get you back home that afternoon. Does that sound possible?"

Francis responded with the first smile Champ had seen on his face. "How could I pass that up? I've not had a pint in months. I will be there."

Champ gave him four dollars in change, and they talked a little longer before Vance and Champ headed back down the road.

Chapter 32

When Champ walked into the Kings Tavern at two o'clock on Sunday, Vance and Morrow were seated at a corner table having a pint of ale and deep in conversation. There was a horse race that day, so the crowd in the pub was thin. Without asking, the barmaid brought Champ a fifteen cent British pint which was twenty ounces. He asked her if she could bring over a tray of bread, cheese and cold cuts for the three of them.

"Francis." Champ asked. "What kind of work were you doing ten years ago in Salem?"

"Actually, I was living in Anderson. I was working for a construction company and we built industrial buildings. I was the site manager of a new plant up near Salem when I met that witch, Virginia. I loved to hunt which put me near the Dare farm one Saturday. I met her while she was out for a walk, and unlucky for me, we struck up a relationship. Virginia led me to think romance could be in the future and I fell for it, most likely the same way the two of you did.

"Unlike you Champ, I arrived here with only a few bucks in my pocket which led to my arrest when I got caught stealing vegetables from a garden. A farmer came along while I was in the stocks. He offered me a job on his farm for about ninety cents a day. I had no choice but to take it. So, I'm here at your generosity and ready to hear you out."

"What is your story James?" Champ asked

"At the time, I was living near Lake Keowee. I was the single dad of a teenager and made my living as a real estate broker. One day I was out canvassing the area for farm acreage. I had a client who wanted property somewhere near the Gap Hill road area, when I made the fatal mistake of driving up Tucker Farm Lane, leading to Virginia's house. My story is the same as yours. She was a beautiful woman. As I have told both of you, soon after arriving here in Williamsburg, I had a run-in with George D'Zing and that's why I work for a tanner. My job really stinks!"

They all shared a good laugh. Vance and Morrow already knew Champ's story, so there was no need to repeat it.

Vance added, "What really pisses me off, is that my boy was left with no one to care for him. I have worried myself sick over these past years. By now, he is grown. I really want to get back home!"

Champ had devised a plan in his mind to leave Williamsburg but felt it prudent only to reveal part of it to Vance and Morrow.

"I think I know the answer to this, but do the two of you want to go with me back to Salem?"

Vance was first to reply. "Champ, I just told you why it is so important to me to return to my time, but if it involves cash, you know that neither Francis or I have any money."

"I realize that. Let me put your minds at ease. If we are able to get away from here, I have the money to finance our trip. And we are in the exact same predicament, so we are brothers in this venture. Agreed?"

They looked at each other and nodded.

"This is exciting, Champ. I just hope you are not getting our hopes up for a lost cause." Francis replied.

"We all want to return to our homes *and* our century. I'll do my best to make this plan work," Champ promised.

"My plan is simple. Next week, I will buy everything we need to make our trip south to Salem, including three good horses, saddles and saddle bags for provisions and clothes. We will need at least one weapon. If either of you have a source for guns, let me know. We will start out with enough food for several days, and we can resupply ourselves along the way."

Vance interrupted, "Champ, if we make it, I think I speak for Francis when I say, we will definitely pay you back."

Francis readily agreed. "As I think about your plan, a few questions come to mind. How far is it to South Carolina? And most importantly, when we arrive, will it be 1791 or 2018?" He grimaced at this last question, as he knew the probable answer.

Champ answered as best he could. "If we were traveling two hundred years from now in a car, I'd say it would be four to five hundred miles to Salem. In the time we presently find ourselves, there are no paved roads. I'm sure the traveling will be difficult. On horseback, it will be at least a month before we arrive in South Carolina, and if we encounter bad weather, it will be miserable. But however difficult, I am of the conviction that it will be worth the attempt."

As an afterthought he added, "In researching a recent book, I learned that the Revolutionary War armies improved the roads for wagons and cannons to travel over and they actually created roads between towns where none had existed previously. We will have to select our route as we go, by connecting with locals and getting directions to the next town.

"I think I can have everything ready by this Saturday. I would like to leave that day. I don't want to wait any longer than that in the fear that Virginia might find out we are planning to leave. Francis, can you get to the livery stable by noon on Saturday?"

When he confirmed that he could, Champ gave him another four dollars to get back to town on Saturday. He motioned to the barmaid and by previous arrangement she handed Champ a small bag of sandwiches, which he gave to Francis.

"I thought some extra food on the way home might be a well-deserved treat for a man who had lived in such a destitute situation for nearly ten years."

Although skeptical, both men agreed with Champ's plan and told him they would be at the livery stable the following Saturday. They were all anxious to hightail it out of that God-forsaken place.

Champ had a lot to do in the next few days and wanted to get started immediately, so he bid farewell to his two new friends.

Chapter 33

Early Monday morning Champ woke to with a loud knock at his boarding house door.

"Who is it?" he called out.

The voice on the other side of the door announced, "It is the Sheriff."

This did not sound good at all. He opened the door and there stood a man with a pistol on each hip and a stern expression on his face. In his hand was a piece of official-looking paper that Champ suppose he was planning to serve him with.

"Sir, are you Mr. Covington?"

"Yes, I'm Covington. Is there a problem?"

"I'm here, sir, to serve you an official notice."

"A notice of what?" he asked.

"It seems that a week ago you provoked Barrister George D'Zing in the privacy of his home. Barrister D'Zing reported that you became violent and he was forced to order you out of his home. He has petitioned the judge to charge you with an invasion of his property."

Champ's first thought was that this represented an absolute corruption of the legal system. D'Zing had his tentacles all over the judge and he was concerned that in his situation he had no power to fight this charge. Champ thought to himself, "this is bullshit!" But he knew better than respond to the sheriff, so he said nothing

The Sheriff continued, "The Barrister has agreed to drop the charge if you will leave Williamsburg and its vicinity by Monday week. If you plan to contest the charges, you will need to appear before the Magistrate. If you will take your leave of Williamsburg and the surrounding countryside, sign here and I will return it to the judge."

That couldn't have played into Champ's plans better. He was not sure if it had been his comment to D'Zing about it being in his best interest if the three abandoned men were not in Virginia's vicinity; or if it had been Virginia herself that had played a hand in this. Either way, Champ did not care. He would be long gone by Monday week, as the sheriff had dictated. Without a word, he signed the paper and shut the door. Vance had been right. This man was malicious.

Later that morning Champ was the first customer at the bank when it opened. He spotted the bank manager, who had kindly offered to take him to dinner. He asked if he could speak with him in private. They went into his office where Champ let him know that he would be withdrawing all his earlier deposits and apologized to him for removing the money so soon after he had opened the account. The bank manager was both surprised and curious as to Champ's reason, so he decided to tell him, at least a partial truth. He mentioned the sheriff's order and D'Zing's petition to the Magistrate. He left out D'Zing's reasons for having him evicted from Williamsburg and the bank manager did not ask. The manager did respond in a hushed tone that he felt the Barrister had far too much power around Williamsburg.

Champ filled out the requisite paperwork and the manager handed him eighteen hundred dollars in small denomination bills and Champ bid him goodbye. One down!

His next stop was the livery stable. He talked with the owner and asked the price for three reliable horses with saddles, bridles and saddle bags.

Since devising his plan he had made several inquiries about the price of a decent horse. So, he was prepared to barter that morning.

The man at the livery made an initial offer. "I will sell you three fine horses for one hundred and fifty dollars apiece. Three saddles including saddle blankets, plus saddle bags and bridles, and throw in three oil skin bags, which you will need for a long journey. All of this will only cost you one hundred dollars per set-up. The total would come to seven hundred and fifty dollars."

Horse trading was an art Champ knew nothing about, but he knew enough to counter liveryman's offer and see where it went. By 2018 standards, that sounded cheap. But Champ's expertise was in law and writing...and a city slicker to boot. This haggling over the price of horses was out of his league.

"I'd like to take a look at the horses, if you don't mind."

He knew a little about horses, but not enough to identify problems other than obvious injuries. He pretended to be scrutinizing each animal. If he took enough time, he might negotiate a better deal. Champ asked the owner to have the stable boy to ride each horse around the ring. He wanted to see whether any were especially spirited and to make sure none of them displayed a limp when it cantered. They had a long ride ahead of them and he needed healthy horses.

He was satisfied that there was not a trouble maker among the three, so he began to barter.

"Did you say seven hundred and fifty dollars?"

"Yes sir."

"I just don't know." Champ I stretched out the words in a measured pace.

"You see, I'm spending two other fellows' money on these horses. I'm sore afraid they would accuse me of spending too much," Champ fibbed.

He wanted to get the price down because he knew they would need money for food and possibly lodging along the way. He was not sure he was right, but he threw out the next bargaining chip anyway.

"You know, these horses look like they got a little age on em'. I'm concerned they might suffer from a long journey like we are planning."

"Tell you what, sir, I could offer you seven hundred twenty-five for the three and that would include everything," offered the livery man.

Champ countered, "I just can't do that my friend. Six fifty would be the best I could do." He was beginning to enjoy this process.

"You strike a hard bargain, sir. At six hundred seventy-five they are yours. I will also throw in a bag of feed for each animal."

Champ gave it one more try. "I'll stick to six fifty and we got a deal."

The owner knew Champ had reached the highest price he was willing to spend and so the liveryman agreed to his price. Champ had saved a hundred dollars.

"Ok, have them ready for me to pick up this Saturday at twelve noon. Now I have one more question. Where might I find rain slickers?"

"At the feed store up on North Henry Street. I'll have everything ready for you on Saturday morning."

As Champ counted out the cash into the liveryman's hand, he noticed a broad smile on the man's face. Maybe he had left some money on the table, after all.

He now had eleven hundred and fifty dollars left for the trip.

Chapter 34

The rest of the week was spent buying food, canteens, tarps, blankets and other necessities. Champ had not used any of the medicine he had brought in the Prince Albert tobacco can. The Aleve especially, would could come in very handy on the trail, since none of them had saddle-hardened backsides.

With all his purchases made, he dropped by the dry goods store to say goodbye to Mr. DeWitt. They had become friendly in the weeks since he had bought the three complete outfits of clothing from him. Champ let him know that he was leaving town. When Mr. DeWitt asked why he was leaving Williamsburg so soon after he had arrived, Champ was truthful about Mr. D'Zing's edict. He figured the more people that knew about this bastard's antics the more trouble he might leave behind for him. As Champ shared his tale, DeWitt's face grew shadowed.

"I am not only sorry to hear that news, Champ, but I am worried for you. Gossip around town is that the Barrister is searching for you."

"Does the gossip indicate why he might be looking for me. According to the Sheriff, if I leave town by Monday week, I have satisfied his complaint."

"I don't know why, but if it were me, I'd stay out of sight. Your story does not surprise me, as he is not well liked in Williamsburg. He has a reputation for being unethical and ruthless."

"I'm a lawyer, Mr. DeWitt, so I know very well what you mean."

They said their goodbyes and Champ headed straight down the back street to the boarding house to collect his belongings. He would spend his last few nights somewhere else. Champ's antenna was up. He had complied with the man's orders to get out of Williamsburg, yet D'Zing reportedly was searching for him. Something fishy was taking place.

****

Although he had heard Virginia's voice shouting at D'Zing, Champ was not aware of the repercussions she had cuffed him with. After Champ left the D'Zing mansion, Virginia had gone ballistic. She had witnessed him being thrown out of the house and heard his threat about her bones. If Champ was able to execute his threat, it would mean the end to Virginia Dare and her time traveling escapades. She would truly be dead!

"George! You know very well that for me to get back to see Mama, I have to take a mortal human being with me. I had planned to use Covington for the return trip back to the farm. You must find him and make up with him anyway you can."

"I will not do that!! He affronted my integrity"

"I don't give a rat's ass about your affronted integrity. You go make that right with Champ." Virginia had obviously picked up a few twenty-first century phrases, as D'Zing looked horrified that such language would come out of the mouth of a lady, much less the lady to which he was betrothed.

"It is too late. I issued an order with the Magistrate for him to vacate Williamsburg by Monday next. The Sheriff has served that order and he has signed it!!"

"And you, George D'Zing, you get on your knees and ask for his forgiveness. I need him to remain here until I am ready to leave. Now!" She pointed her finger toward the door and evaporated from the room.

George had known very well where Champ was all day. D'Zing wanted Champ out of town and was only pretending to be looking for him. Champ had figured all along that D'Zing saw him as competition for Virginia. And he did not want Virginia to continue going back and forth to South Carolina for long periods of time. Getting rid of Champ was his way of ending that practice. Virginia no longer knew where Francis Morrow or James Vance were, so Champ was her only ticket back.

After leaving the mercantile, Champ knew that D'Zing was looking for him, but did not know why. However, he did know that if Virginia came hunting him it would lead to some serious problems. Even worse, if George found out she was looking, he could trump up charges and have him thrown in prison. All this was pure speculation on Champ's part, but just the thought of any of it happening frightened him.

He would not take any chances. He found a granary storeroom near the livery and had his effects delivered there. He would sleep on grain sacks for the next few nights. No one would look for him there.

Chapter 35

At precisely noon on Saturday Champ met Vance and Morrow at the livery stable where the owner had saddled up the horses and had them ready to go.

Although they noticed Champ moving his belongings from the granary, they did not ask why, and he did not tell them. It took longer than he wanted, but they finally had their supplies loaded properly on the horses and were prepared to leave Williamsburg. Champ could not wait to get out of town and beyond the reaches of Virginia Dare.

Just as a precaution, he had told the boarding house proprietor that he was heading for New York, and the same was told to the livery stable owner. They must have looked a sight, because the horses could not have carried one more item.

If D'Zing was indeed looking for Champ, this misinformation may confuse him, but he knew it wouldn't fool Virginia.

Still speculating about Virginia's intentions, he wondered what would happen if she came looking for him, maybe even down the road after they left town. She would not only find him, but she would also find Vance and Morrow. They had gotten to the edge of town and Champ stopped and told the two he needed a commitment.

"What I'm saying here is pure speculation, but we all know that Virginia cannot be trusted. Should she find us and try to lure one of us away with a promise to take us back to Salem, I recommend, at all costs, we stick together and not fall for her trickery again. Are we in this for the long haul together?" Champ asked.

Both Morrow and Vance vehemently confirmed this pledge. Given the amount of time each of them had been abandoned in Williamsburg, he probably wouldn't have needed to worry.

The only one he had been honest with about his real travel plans, was Mr. DeWitt. He asked advice about traveling south. DeWitt advised him to take the Richmond road that would at first take them in a northwest direction. The reason for this detour was because the road took them beside a big river with no bridges to cross it until they reached Richmond. That was roughly a three-day ride, and at that point there was a good bridge that would allow them to head south. This direction would also make anyone they encountered, believe they were heading north. Champ then asked DeWitt to claim ignorance of his whereabouts and requested that he not tell anyone he was even traveling out of town.

****

It was February and daylight hours were short. They had ridden maybe twenty miles when they saw an old barn not far off the road. There was no farm house nearby, so Champ suggested that they bed down in the barn where it would be warmer and out of the elements. He was also thinking of animal predators. Vance had found two pistols and a rifle for thirty dollars before they had left town, so they felt fairly secure.

They made good time on Sunday, without incident. But on Monday morning a mixture of cold rain and sleet made traveling difficult, and they did not make nearly the miles of the previous day. They lucked out and found another abandoned barn to sleep in. The slickers had been a god-send that day. Barns would prove to be one of their primary shelters along the trip. Even when farms were occupied, most farmers did not object to them using the barns for shelter. Sometimes they would offer to feed horses or do minor chores in exchange for the dry hay on which to sleep.

Precipitation in varying forms of rain, sleet and snow continued to plague them for several days. On the morning of their fourth day, they rounded a bend in the muddy, rutted road, and were delighted to see signs announcing they had arrived in Richmond, Virginia. Because of the treacherous weather, and long days in the saddle for three inexperienced horsemen, Champ suggested they find a small inn and stay for the night. He still had over one thousand dollars and did not mind spending some of it for an occasional bed with sheets and a hot meal. They enjoyed Richmond Inn's log fire and treated themselves to a pint of ale before heading to their beds. Champ had taken a private room while Vance and Morrow insisted on using the bunkhouse to save a few dollars. The Inn had a stable, so their tired horses were fed and groomed by the stable boys.

After nearly a week on the road, the food and feather bed were pure luxury to Champ. He looked forward to a good night's sleep. But it was not to be. Sometime in the wee hours of the night, Virginia appeared in his dreams. He was tossing and turning as she was telling him to wake up, she wanted to talk with him. He was in that middle ground between deep sleep and wakefulness, as he felt someone poking him. He opened his eyes but could see nothing in the black room. Then he heard her voice. It made him shudder. Was he still dreaming or was she making an appearance in my boarding room? He got out of bed and lit his oil lamp. Champ looked around the small room, but saw nothing, so he decided it must have been his constant concern over her finding him that had invaded his dreams.

Then he heard her speak to him again.

"Champ, why did you leave Williamsburg without speaking to me?"

He could not believe, first that she had again invaded his mind, but second, that she actually asked him that question. He wanted to scream, 'you bitch' but he knew better than to take on a losing battle with a ghost.

However, he could not help responding gruffly, "Miss Dare, if you want to speak with me, do me the dignity of showing yourself."

In a moment she began to manifest herself in the only chair available. She was sitting comfortably in the chair and looking straight at him with those beautiful brown eyes. She had on a winter dress with a heavy coat and tall leather boots. And her lustrous chestnut hair was hidden under a stylish wool hat.

"I left Williamsburg because your fiancée ran me out of town, as I am quite certain you are aware. Just what is it you want with me that is so important that you must wake me in the middle of the night?"

Virginia applied the same coyness she had used on him before. "It is not what it seems, Champ. George forced me to not have any contact with you, or he would make my life miserable. He surmised that you serve as the catalyst between my remaining in Williamsburg or traveling back to my farm in South Carolina."

"So, George knows that I'm your ticket to go back home? Isn't that right?"

"Yes." She answered simply.

"Well, he must figure you will have no choice but to stay with him? And you don't like not having all the power in any situation, do you? How am I doing so far, Miss Dare? I think I have you pretty well nailed."

Virginia did not reply immediately. Finally, she adopted a 'helpful tone'.

"Dear Champ, I merely wanted to warn you about what's going on. George and I had a big fight. I told him that if he did not find you and allow you to live in Williamsburg, I was going to disappear and never see him again. He must have taken my threat seriously, and he is now out looking for you. He was told that you were headed for New York, but he doubted it, and is looking for you on the road headed south towards Salem."

"You know as well as I do, Virginia, if I come back to Williamsburg, the Barrister would find some reason to have me imprisoned or impoverished." I was making veiled reference to Vance and Morrow, to gauge her reaction.

"Virginia, I am certain you know the tragedies that have befallen the other two men you brought to Williamsburg to facilitate your ghostly travels. You and Mr. D'Zing made it impossible for one of the men to get work. The other one nearly starved to death and spent a week in the stockades for stealing a few vegetables. I personally am abhorred by your behavior and I know I speak for the other two men when I say that I have lost interest in you."

Champ could see tears forming in her eyes. Although she looked genuinely sorrowful, he decided this must be yet another one of her clever tactics to achieve her own goals. This time, her tears had no effect on him.

"I never intended for this to happen, Champ. George has more sway in Williamsburg than even the judges. I'm just a woman with no influence. I did not inherit my family's estate and have no money. I have been under his power for a number of years and don't seem to have the strength to leave him. My mother does not approve of him and does not want to live under his roof in Williamsburg. You have seen my farm in Salem. There are no comforts in that house. If it were not for my mother, I would never go back to the farm."

Bingo! Now he knew why her mother would not travel with her.

"Virginia, you can cut the sob story. It no longer has power to move me. I will tell you this, I may never get back to 2018, but I'm going south to where I belong. At least I can live out my life without the fear of a bastard like George D'Zing making life hell. Now get out of my room and never come calling on me again...as a ghost of a human being!"

Early the next morning after a warm breakfast of boiled eggs, bread, cheese and hot coffee, Champ headed to pay their bill. The two rooms and supper cost him twelve dollars. Breakfast was a little extra, but well worth it. At this rate, his money would be sufficient for the trip, and then some.

When he was settling his tab, he overheard the desk clerk talking about four men that had arrived very early that morning demanding to know if they had given shelter to a man traveling from Williamsburg. He told about one of the men who had behaved rudely to the barmaid. When he described the man, I knew it had to be D'Zing. The clerk told the men he had not seen a man traveling alone that had come from Williamsburg and so they headed out.

The three of them had agreed when they arrived at the Inn, that no mention would be made of where they traveled from or where they had lived. However, now Champ knew D'Zing was looking for him, it gave all of them cause for concern. They agreed it would be safer if they adopted aliases as they traveled.

The three men could not leave Richmond fast enough, and there was almost an audible sigh as they crossed the river and headed south. Their plan was to travel about twenty miles each day. On good days that was ten hours in the saddle. By now they were becoming experienced horsemen...at least that's what they thought.

They were fortunate with weather that day and at noon they decided to give their horses an opportunity to graze. As they prepared to dismount and have a bite to eat, Champ noticed four riders in the distance heading in their direction. The man in the lead road a stately white stallion. Instinct told Champ that man was D'Zing. They must have headed south after leaving the Richmond Inn and when they did not overtake Champ, were now heading back.

Champ warned the other two. Morrow had indicated he was a sharp shot, so Champ handed him the rifle and told him to hide in the thicket about twenty yards back and watch him. If Champ pointed at him, he was to hold a bead on D'Zing's head. Champ would do the rest. The lawyer in him was emerging.

He did not want a confrontation, but he needed to face off with D'Zing and get it over with.

When D'Zing got close enough to eyeball Champ he recognized him and picked up his pace. Vance and Champ turned to their right and off the road into the meadow. The thicket where Morrow was hiding ran the length of the meadow behind them. Vance and Champ faced the four men that were fast approaching. They did not draw their guns. They merely sat atop their horses, with hands planted on their saddle horns and waited. D'Zing and his cronies drew their horses up to within ten feet of Champ and Vance, and stopped.

"Covington, what are you doing so far out of Williamsburg?"

"Now that's a good one Barrister, since you ran me out of town. As far as that goes, I could ask you the same."

"Well, I have changed my mind and want you to come back and live in Williamsburg. I won't give you any problems."

It was all Champ could do not to laugh in his face.

"Now George, why would you possibly want me to come back? What unearthly thing could have possibly changed your mind in the past week?" Champ decided his answer was going to be one for the books and could hardly wait to hear how he might spin Virginia's directive to bring him back.

"I just thought it was the Christian thing to do."

This time he did laugh. He couldn't help himself and he was tempted to let him know that Virginia had paid him a visit the previous night.

"You cannot be serious George! There are three men who have been marooned in a time warp. Your lovely fiancée, Virginia, used us for her transportation, and then abandoned us in your backyard. You don't really want us near your beautiful Virginia, do you? After all, she had made overtures to each one of us over the past decade. What if she were to change her mind and pick one of us, over you? How would that be?"

George was becoming nervous. He knew his three men did not have a clue what we were talking about, but Champ watched his hand as it made a slight move toward his pistol.

"All three of you can come back. I will make it right for all of you. You can believe that." Champ was thinking that Virginia must have him by his balls. And her story about his domination over her was holding less water than it did in the middle of the previous night.

"I'll tell you George, what I believe, is that Virginia has threatened you and you are petrified that if you don't do her bidding, she will leave you too. Did I get that correct?"

"Are you calling me a *liar*?" George's face was growing red. This was the second time Champ had observed his quick temper get out of control.

"No George, I'm not calling you liar. What I am saying is that we are not going to fall into your little trap. We do not want to come back to your town. It stinks. We are going our way, and I suggest you do the same."

At that moment D'Zing turned and said to his men.

"Alright men, let's take 'em in."

With that, the three henchmen drew their pistols and pointed them at Champ and Vance.

"Now, gentlemen, before you do anything rash, are you familiar with a squirrel shooter? If you are, you know that they rarely miss their target.

Champ could see that this made D'Zing and his men nervous. His hand was shaking as it poised over his pistol.

"Well, let me explain a squirrel shooter to you. Not only do they *never* miss their target, but if you look to your left, there is one standing right there with his squirrel rifle pointed at your head." Champ indicated in Morrow's direction.

"He has never missed a squirrel, George. So, I suggest you and your thugs turn around and head back to

Williamsburg before you get your silver-haired wig blown off your pompous head."

D'Zing could see Morrow in the bushes and knew he was the likely target. His face continued to grow red, but his legal training had made him a survivor and knew when he was beat.

"If you ever cross my path again, I'll string you up on the gallows and let you rot! Let's go men."

With that, they turned their horses and headed in the direction of Williamsburg at a gallop.

When D'Zing was out of sight, Morrow slapped Champ on the back and told him that he was one cool SOB. It might have looked like that to Morrow, but underneath he was sweating bullets.

Champ still was not sure D'Zing wouldn't return, so they headed out to get as much distance between them as possible. Just after dusk They spotted a farmhouse with a large barn. The farmer graciously let them bed down in the loft. It made Champ feel better that they were on a farm that was occupied.

Just as they were about to pull their meager rations from the oil sacks, the farmer appeared at the entrance to the barn, holding the most beautiful pork shoulder Champ had ever seen. The farmer had slaughtered a hog that afternoon and was now offering the weary travelers a portion large enough to last them for several days. They thanked the farmer and offered to pay for the meat. He would have none of it, so they built a fire and roasted the pork on a large stick. Three hours later they had the finest meal they had ever tasted. What a day it had been!

Chapter 36

They arrived in Salem, North Carolina about mid-April. Champ estimated they had traveled over two hundred and seventy-five miles. During that time, they had only stayed at one Inn. Farmers and townspeople along the way had been very gracious to the three weary travelers. Thus, Champ had been able to preserve most of his money.

Now it was time for them to splurge on a soft bed, a bath and a good hot meal. They found a very nice Inn at the center of the square. They quoted Champ five dollars apiece including supper and breakfast. That was an extravagance he was willing to pay for.

The Inn was bustling with activity. The dining room and pub were overflowing with patrons. After a good long soak in the tub, they dressed in their best clothes and were pleased to find a table for three near the fireplace. They each ordered a pint of ale and chatted before asking to be served. Champ sensed an atmosphere among the patrons that was almost frenetic but could not exactly put his finger on why.

Morrow grew impatient as he waited for a second pint of ale and headed up to the bar. When he came back, he too had that odd excitement on his face.

"Everyone at the bar is saying that President Washington is staying here tonight. He is headed to South Carolina. Can you believe that? Here they were, three twenty-first century guys, and they might get to see their country's founding father!"

If they ever doubted what century they were presently in, tonight there was no question. Champ chuckled and shared his humorous thought with Vance and Morrow.

"Someday, there will be a sign at the front door of this 'historic building' that says: 'George Washington slept here'. How cool is that to actually be in the same Inn tonight?"

They laughed too, at the memory of that frequent claim about all the places Washington had slept.

"Perhaps our names will be on that plaque too. You think?" Vance chortled. They all laughed so hard that the tables around them stopped their conversation to hear what was so funny.

They speculated that the President would take his breakfast in that dining room in the morning, so their plan was to be in the dining room early enough to perhaps catch a glimpse of the great man.

Evidently, they were not the only ones with that idea, as the dining room was crowded at seven-thirty the next morning. However, they did find the same corner table near the fireplace. Around eight o'clock, Washington entered the room with another man and headed toward a table where two others were already seated.

Champ, Morrow and Vance watched his every move, as unobtrusively as possible. He had ordered griddle cakes and bacon. They finished their breakfast and dawdled over several more cups of coffee. Finally, they could wait no longer to get on the road, so they left the dining room. Champ would have loved to shake President Washington's hand, but thought better of the impulse. Right then he was wishing he had snuck his iPhone in his pocket instead of that tobacco tin. A selfie with Washington! Now, that would be hard to explain in 2018.

In the past two months, Champ had seen both Jefferson and Washington. Mindboggling!

As they left Salem, they estimated that they were about half way home. How ironic was that thought! When they arrived home, the actual location of their homes would still be over two hundred years in the future...unless Champ's plan worked.

****

Saddle sores no longer plagued them as the distance from Williamsburg grew. In the next few weeks they would travel through Charlotte, Spartanburg, Pleasantdale (which is now Greenville), Pickens and then at last, Salem.

His money had held up well and they lacked for almost nothing. Although they kept to their schedule of ten-hour days on their horses, they treated them well, provided adequate feed and water and took them to livery stables to check their shoes as they rode through small towns. So, their horses had made the trip without a problem.

Three weeks later, they would cross the Keowee River and head toward what they had known as Salem. Although they had known many of the names of the towns in the South, very little looked familiar.

Champ could sense the apprehension increasing as the three men neared Salem. It was late in the afternoon, so he suggested they stay in and abandoned shack he had spotted.

It was the first week of April, and the chilly winds of spring were blowing through their slickers. The only humorous note of the day was that none of them recognized Salem. In 1791 it was nothing more than a crossroad with a few farmhouses and a small general store. Before Champ's travels with Virginia, nearly three months earlier, there had been a bank, several churches, schools, a firehouse and an Ace Hardware. On this day, the only road to Salem was a muddy, rutted path.

It had only been a few years before 1791 that the white settlers had reached a truce with the Cherokees. Indians were still in the vicinity, but we did not see any on our ride into town.

An abandoned shack was certainly not the accommodations they'd had in Salem, *North* Carolina, but still, they enjoyed their meal of country ham, boiled eggs and hard bread they had purchased in Pickens the day before. This first night in Salem, brought mixed emotions.

The next morning, the wind had died, and after a pot of coffee, they saddled up and headed towards the general store to ask directions to Gap Hill road. The proprietor looked puzzled. He was not familiar with that road name and informed the three men that many roads in the area did not have proper names. Champ told him we were looking for the Dare family farm and asked if he knew where it was located.

"The Dare farm, that's down this road maybe four or five miles. They got a shiny new sign on the road that says Tucker Farm." He chuckled. "Strange why they named it Tucker. Anyways, just follow the lane down about a mile, and you will see the farmhouse."

Champ asked, "Does the Dare family ever come in to town?"

"No, no, can't say that I have seen the wife lately. She used to come in with her pretty little daughter about once a week. Husband came in every few days, but a bear kill't him a piece back. He was a fine man. Fought in the war, you know. Told me he got him a bunch of Red Coats."

They thanked the shopkeeper and headed in the direction he had indicated. They had traveled nearly an hour when they came to a spot where they needed cross the Keowee River again. This meant they were getting within a mile of Tucker Farm Lane. Champ wasn't sure about the other guys, but since it had been only a few months since he had been down that road, he felt he would recognize the driveway.

****

Their trip from Williamsburg had taken just over six weeks. During that time neither Vance nor Morrow had questioned how Champ thought he could get them back to 2018. Perhaps they were afraid to ask. To a large degree, they were just glad to have Williamsburg and George D'Zing far behind them, regardless of the year they ended up in.

But Champ did have a plan. A plan he had run through his mind hundreds of times over the course of their travels. Now, as they approached Tucker Farm Lane, he thought it might be time to reveal what he had in mind, but it still didn't feel like right. Champ wanted to check out the farmhouse first.

He knew it was only a mile own that lane, but after all the traveling they had done together, that last mile seemed like an excruciatingly long ride.

At last the woods opened into a small valley where the trees had been cleared near the farmhouse and the winter wheat was being cut. He could see four young men using scythes to cut the wheat.

They tethered their horses at the hitching post near the house. Champ had goose bumps as he stepped onto the porch. He had no clue who would be standing there when the door opened.

He knocked and after a few minutes an old woman, who he recognized as Virginia's mother, opened the door. She wore that same blue floor-length frock with the matching bonnet. She was tall and angular. He could see the resemblance between mother and daughter. She looked at him for a moment and asked in a rather weak voice,

"May I help you?" Champ figured she was trying to determine if he was who she thought.

"Mrs. Dare, pardon my intrusion, however, my friends and I came on a very important errand. My name is Champ Covington. I believe you are the mother of Miss Virginia Dare?"

"Yes, Virginia is my daughter. Why are you here on my farm?"

Champ hesitated, not knowing exactly how to explain his problem to her. He had been told she knew that Virginia came and went through time, so he had to assume that process did not need explaining to her.

In his most tender voice Champ began, "Mrs. Dare, my errand concerns Virginia. Do you think we could sit out here on the porch and I will explain my purpose?"

"I suppose we could but excuse me one minute." She disappeared into the house.

Champ asked Vance and Morrow to trust him for a few more minutes and told them this was the second half of his plan that he would explain shortly. He needed them to give him some private time with Mrs. Dare and suggested they walk down to the old oak tree near the wheat field until he called them back. He thought about his truck that had been left in the barn. But of course, as things stood, the truck would not be in the barn until 2018.

Mrs. Dare came back to the door and handed Champ three glasses of water on a tray. He took two glasses to Francis and James. It was cool and refreshing and tasted just like the water Virginia had given him months ago…no, two hundred years ago!

"Now tell me about Virginia, Mr. Covington. Is there trouble? Is she ill?"

"I suppose you could say there is trouble, but she is not ill.

"You may not remember, but several months ago I was here at Christmas time for a visit with Virginia and I left you a small gift."

She hesitated as if not sure to admit the situation. Finally, she spoke.

"Yes, I know who you are. You are one of *those* men."

"By that, do you mean, one of the men who travel with Virginia?" I asked cautiously.

"Yes. Yes, she took you with her and I have not seen her since. Where did you travel to?" she asked coyly.

Still trying to be gentle with the old woman, Champ continued, "Mrs. Dare, I believe you *know* she is in Williamsburg. She is unhappy because she cannot come home to you. Both you and I know how she travels back and forth, don't we?"

The old woman stared down at her weathered hands and said nothing, so Champ persisted. "As you know, she took me along. When we left, the year was 2018 and now as you and I sit here it is 1791. Mr. George D'Zing, I understand, is her fiancée. He is a very powerful lawyer in Williamsburg and he did not like having me there, so he forced me to leave. As I'm sure you are aware, I was your daughter's ticket back to you in South Carolina."

Now she was curious. Her head jerked up and she asked, "Then how did you get here?"

"I and the two men with me today have all been transported by Virginia back to 1791 Williamsburg and abandoned there by your daughter. We have ridden for nearly two months to get back Salem."

"But Mr. Covington, why did you come all the way back here?"

"Mrs. Dare, as I just told you, when I left here, the year was 2018. I very much want to go back to the century in which I belong and so do the other two men." Champ gestured to Vance and Morrow, waiting patiently under the nearby tree.

"One of the men was abandoned by your daughter in Williamsburg over ten years ago and the other gentleman nearly seven years ago. Mrs. Dare, I know you miss your daughter. Just the same as these men miss their families, and as I do. *That* is why I am here. I need your help to correct what Virginia has done to us."

"But why me?" she asked, sounding fearful.

"Mrs. Dare, to be candid with you, Virginia told me that you also have the same power she does to travel through time. She told me that while you have the ability to follow her to Williamsburg, you prefer not to leave this farm."

"Mr. Covington, what is that you want from me. As you can see I'm very old."

"I need you to help the three of us get back to the twenty-first century. "

"But I cannot do that."

The gentle tone I had wanted to maintain, was becoming more difficult.

"Mrs. Dare, why can you not do this for us? Is it because you *cannot,* or because you *will* not?"

"No, no, I cannot just send you back to your own time. We would have to go back to Williamsburg and then forward to where you came from. I cannot do all that travel. I am old."

She looked truly frightened at the thought.

"Mrs. Dare, you may be old, but I have every confidence you have the ability to manage this transport for us. After all, we are in this predicament because of your daughter. Do you not owe that to us?"

"I cannot do this; and I *will* not do it! You will have to find another way."

Now Champ's blood was beginning to simmer. He tried not to show it, but he knew she could do what he was asking, and whether it was because she didn't want to leave the farm or didn't want to upset her daughter, he did not know. And he did not care. She had left him no options.

"Mrs. Dare, let me be straightforward. First, your daughter is frantic to return home to you and at this moment has not been able to make her way back.

"Second, the three of us men are equally desperate to return to our homes and our century. I was hopeful that you would be cooperative and willing to help us. However, you leave me no choice. If you refuse to help us get back to our own time, I will go up to your family cemetery and dig up Virginia's grave. I will crush her bones and throw them to the wind. You know very well that she requires her grave to travel through the centuries. When I scatter her bones, it will guarantee she will never be able to return and you will never see your daughter again. I am sorry to have to resort to this threat, but I am a desperate man."

Mrs. Dare was visibly shaken by Champ's threat. He could see in her eyes that she knew he was right, and his threat had not been an idle one. She sat looking at her hands again for such a long time that feared she had fallen asleep. Finally, she replied,

"If I'm agreeable to this, do you and the other two men promise never, ever to see my Virginia again?"

Champ thought that was an interesting request. "I can guarantee you, Mrs. Dare, that we will keep that promise. Your daughter is a beautiful woman, but she has caused irreparable damage to each of our lives. None of us have any desire to court your daughter ever again.

"I have one additional promise, Mrs. Dare. And this is a promise, not a threat. If you should leave us stranded in Williamsburg, at least one of us will make our way back here to Salem and we will follow through with the desecration of Virginia's grave. Do you understand?"

Mrs. Dare had tears in her eyes. Champ hated this part of his plan, but it had to be done. He particularly hated Virginia for causing her mother so much pain.

She sighed heavily. "I will do as you ask because I need my daughter. Be here precisely at noon tomorrow. Leave your horses in the stalls of the barn. You will not see them again. They will be my payment for this inconvenience." I could now see the spunk in the old woman, and realized she was not as feeble as she had made herself out to be.

Chapter 37

It promised to be a warm evening, so they camped out beside the creek that followed Tucker Lane into the farm. They found a spot under a Rhododendron thicket and remained out of sight for the night. It was now that Champ explained the remainder of his plan to James and Francis. The risky part was the chance that Mrs. Dare would leave them marooned in Williamsburg for a second time. He explained, it was really their only chance to get back home, to their own century.

Morrow's reaction was immediate. "I will not take the chance! Even if it means that I have to live the rest of my natural life in the 1700's. I will never go back to that wretched place."

Vance was skeptical and hesitant, just as Champ had expected. But he was a thinker and pondered Champ's plan before he said anything.

"I don't like this any more than you do Francis, but I really need to get home to my family and I'm willing to do anything to see my son again."

After much discussion and persuasion, Morrow was finally convinced. Each of the men lapsed into silence, lost in his own thoughts. Champ realized that returning to 2018 would be the easiest for him, as much would not have changed. He wondered how Morrow and Vance might fare and promised himself that he would keep in touch with the two men.

****

They were at the barn before noon and had stabled their horses. There were oats and hay, so they rubbed them down for the last time and fed them. The three horses had become trusted friends throughout this journey, and the three each realized they would miss their steeds.

They walked over to the house and found Mrs. Dare sitting on the porch waiting. A wagon and driver pulled up to the porch. Vance helped her climb into the seat beside the driver and the three men settled in the back.

When they arrived at the cemetery, the driver asked if he should wait. She told him to be back by three o'clock. Champ introduced James and Francis to her. She took long looks at them but said nothing. Champ felt she was trying to remember these two other suiters of her daughter. They followed Mrs. Dare over near the graves.

Finally, she broke her silence.

"The three of you have experienced this transition before so you know what to expect. We will all lie on my grave and hold hands. Hang on tight to each other as you did with Virginia. Keep your eyes tightly closed, for as we approach the bands of light that separate the centuries, that light will be as bright as if you were looking directly into the sun. Listen for my instruction on when to open your eyes. If you have a question, please ask now."

Champ did have a question. "Where will we touch down in Williamsburg? I have no desire to run into Barrister D'Zing."

"And neither do I!" she retorted. Virginia had certainly been right about her mother's dislike for D'Zing.

Mrs. Dare continued, "We will arrive in the old Bruton Parish Episcopal Church cemetery. It is where my great grandmother's grave is located. We will also immediately depart from that location, so do not wander away."

'Oh, you can count on that!' Champ thought. And then he added another question. "And it will be the year 2018 when we come back to this spot later today?"

"That is correct Mr. Covington."

Actually, that would turn out not to be true, not completely, anyway.

****

All three of them were a bundle of nerves as they lay down on Mrs. Dare's grave. Champ held hands with Mrs. Dare on her right while Vance and Morrow joined her on her left. As they lay there in total silence, the only sound was a small insect buzzing near Champ's ear.

Soon he felt a tremor under his back. He couldn't tell if they were still visible at that point, but if they were, what a sight that would be...four bodies levitating above a grave.

Again, Champ felt no wind. Soon the darkness of space reached them as the hues of the earth were left behind. Since their eyes were closed, they felt this rather than saw it, but it was just as real. The experiences of the astronauts could not possibly have exceeded what they were now feeling.

In what seemed like an instant, Mrs. Dare told them to prepare for a gentle landing on the cemetery grounds. The first leg of the trip was over. Champ stole a glance at his two companions and they both had smiles pasted on their faces. All around them were moss-covered tombstones and tall obelisks, reserving for all time the names of our ancestors. As promised, the grave they had landed on was Mrs. Dare's great grandmother, Mary Dare. Champ tried but could not read the dates.

Mrs. Dare reminded the men not to move. Within less than thirty seconds, she instructed them to lie down, close their eyes and join hands. As Champ grabbed the old woman's hand, he hoped with all he had that this would be the last time he departed from Williamsburg, Virginia.

"It is time again to travel," Mrs. Dare announced and then mumbled words similar to those Virginia had used.

Champ wouldn't admit this time travel was enjoyable, but it did not scare the shit out of him like it had the first time. He was just extremely grateful that he would never have to do it again!

Chapter 38

When they touched back down on the grave of Mrs. Dare, at the cemetery in South Carolina, no words could describe Champ's feelings. He was both exhilarated and frightened. What if it hadn't worked and he was still in another time zone?

He had to ask, "Mrs. Dare, we are back in 2018, aren't we?"

"*You* are Mr. Covington. But Mr. Vance and Mr. Morrow are not with us."

Panic hit Champ. What had he done? Had he left them in 1791? Did the travel back somehow not work for them? Champ looked around and they were nowhere in sight.

There was panic in his voice. "What have you done with them? Why aren't they with us? We have to go back, we have to go back right now!" he screamed.

"Calm, Mr. Covington. They have returned to the date and time *they* left the farm. Mr. Morrow left in 2008, and Mr. Vance in 2012. Virginia told them, as she did you, that they would return back to the farm on the same date they left, and that is why you do not see them here with us."

This information made Champ's head spin. How could he trust that she was telling him the truth? Would he never see them again? True to her daughter's abilities, Mrs. Dare could also evidently read minds. For she attempted to assure him of my friends' safe arrival in their own time.

"Mr. Covington, I promise you that I have delivered your friends back to their own time, just as I promised you I would."

Champ had to believe her. He could not prove otherwise...at least until he could get to the internet and look up the two men. And that is precisely what he intended to do!

He had been gone three months, but back in time, two hundred and twenty-even years in the past. Of course, there was no wagon waiting for them. That wagon had come back at three o'clock to the cemetery in April 1791 to pick up Mrs. Dare. It had long since disappeared into dust.

It dawned on Champ that he needed somehow to get Mrs. Dare down the hillside and back to her home.

"Thank you, Mrs. Dare." he told her sincerely. "Let me run down the hill. I will bring my truck up here and you can ride back to the house with me."

When they had put their horses in the barn before noon that day, the year was 1791. Now, this afternoon, as he approached the barn, weeds had grown up in front of the doors, just as he remembered seeing them the first time he was with Virginia. With great anticipation and not a little skepticism, he struggled to pull back one of the weather-beaten doors. When he finally was able to get the door open and saw his beloved Ford F-150, he let out a yell of excitement. Never had he loved that truck more than today. It was the first validation that he was truly back in the twenty-first century. There it sat, the same as he had left it three months earlier…or had it been only hours ago? The key was still on the seat. Champ put it in the ignition and the engine came alive.

He drove back up the hill and helped Mrs. Dare into the seat beside him. Champ sensed that riding in such a 'new-fangled' automobile frightened her.

"Mrs. Dare, I know that none of this situation was of your making, but I want you to know how much all three of us appreciate your helping us escape that nightmare. We were not meant to live back in colonial times."

The farmhouse looked much like it had when we left it earlier that day in 1791. Champ asked Mrs. Dare if there was anything she needed from the grocery store. If she did he would gladly bring it to her. She politely declined. He helped her out of the truck and without another word, she walked slowly toward the house. She turned slightly before entering the door and nodded to him. Champ knew he would never see her again.

****

He was absolutely giddy as he bought a few groceries and then headed to his cabin. He remembered Virginia telling him that when he returned, things would be the same as he had left them. It would be as if he had never been away. She was right. Champ's cabin looked untouched.

It was Saturday afternoon, so he rode up to Bob's Place. He was hoping Big Bongo would be there. He had missed both his friend and his dog, Sam.

Sure enough, there was Big Bongo holding court and consuming beer. He turned around and was astounded to see Champ.

"Well I'll be a monkey's uncle!"

No one except Bongo knew about his adventure, so he grabbed a beer for Champ and they headed outside to the yard.

"You just left! Why are you back so soon? Did that blue lady kick you out?" he asked.

Champ allowed a grin and said. "Not exactly, Bongo. But it's a very, very long story, and I plan to write a book about my experiences. Tell you what, I'll give you the first copy when it is published, and *then* you will know what happened to me." Champ was teasing him, but also did not want to get into the details of his misadventure in the yard of Bob's Place.

"Bongo, can I get Sam? I really miss that old hound dog."

Just then a howl came from the door of the bar. Champ turned and saw his aging coonhound lumbering towards him. He swooped Sam into his arms and let him slobber all over his face. What a wonderful feeling that was!

Chapter 39

It took about two weeks for his brain to stop spinning, so that he could begin to settle down. He met with Little Tom Tatum and heard the end of Tom's story about his father. Big Tom Tatum's life had had a sad ending and Champ hated that for Little Tom. But he knew as he resumed writing, he would pull out all the good things that Little Tom had told him about his father, so they would not be overshadowed by the tragedy.

Finally, Champ had no distractions. Over the next several months, he would seriously begin work on the book he had originally set out to write.

During the six weeks he had been on horseback and surviving in the backwoods of the colonial South, Champ had toughened into the best shape of his life. However, since returning, he had quickly lost those toned muscles. "Perhaps they were still in 1791," he chuckled to himself. Well, the only way to get them back in 2018 was to work at it. So, he made a commitment to get out on his bike for several hours every day.

One day, after a long ride on his bike through the back roads of The Dark Corner, he made the final turn into my driveway, Champ was surprised to see a man sitting on the edge of his porch. There was something different about this man. And Champ surmised that he must have walked to the cabin from Gap Hill Road, because there was neither a bicycle or a car. When he got enough to see the man's features, he was STUNNED!

There sitting on Champ's front stoop sat Barrister George D'Zing.

The End

Epilog

Virginia Dare had told each of the three men before departing on their adventure, that they would return back to the farm in Salem at the same time and date they had departed, and it would seem as though they had never left. This was certainly the case with Champ Covington. Even the loaf bread he had left on the kitchen counter was still fresh. His life would continue without interruption. However, it bothered him that he could never find out for certain that James and Francis had made it home safely. He would go on to write a book about Big Tom Tatum's life and tragic death. Not surprisingly, his next book was the one you have just read. *'The Authors Woman'*

*****